4 F.B. Fair

CH⟩ EL.

β

H

H

THE DYING TREE

With the railroad pushing into Indian territory, the peace treaty between the Sioux and the white men is broken. Sioux warriors attack railroad surveyors and only Civil War veteran Mike Wilson escapes. Serving his own purposes, the railroad boss schemes for an Indian war, which triggers an explosive and violent reaction from the local tribes. Now there would be war lasting for many years, drenching the prairie grass with the blood of Indians and white men alike.

EDWARD THOMSON

THE DYING TREE

Complete and Unabridged

LINFORD
Leicester

First published in Great Britain in 2000

Originally published in paperback as
Drums of the Prairie by P. Lawrence

First Linford Edition
published 2007

British Library CIP Data

Thomson, Edward, *1919 –*
    The dying tree.—Large print ed.—
Linford western library
1. Western stories
2. Large type books
I. Title
823.9′14 [F]
788 3015
ISBN 978–1–84617–626–5

Published by
F. A. Thorpe (Publishing)
Anstey, Leicestershire

Set by Words & Graphics Ltd.
Anstey, Leicestershire
Printed and bound in Great Britain by
T. J. International Ltd., Padstow, Cornwall

This book is printed on acid-free paper

1

From where he sat beneath the spreading branches of the cottonwood old Caleb could see clear down the trail to Morgan's Creek. It was a thin, rutted, dusty trail, winding like a bleached snake over the parched ground. Past Morgan's Creek it twisted its way over the prairie towards Kansas and the West. To the east it wound through the foothills and wooded hills of Missouri, meeting up with the main stageroutes serving the East.

Little traffic used the trail now though, back in the days before civil war had set the North and South at each other's throats, the heavy wagons of west-bound settlers had creaked and groaned their way towards the promised lands of California and Oregon. Those same wagons had marked the trail others were to follow, their big,

1

iron-rimmed wheels grinding the life from the grass and leaving a path all could see.

Now the wagons no longer used this route, preferring the easier path to the south through Oklahoma or veering north through Nebraska and, aside from the two-weekly stage and an occasional party of riders, the trail lay baking under the hot sun, alone and deserted.

Caleb sighed as he thought about it. He turned, looking at the clapboard shack and store which he had built with his own hands. He had built it when Morgan's Creek was the camping ground for the west-bound settlers and had stocked it with leather goods, powder and ball for the old percussion cap weapons, cotton goods for the women, molasses, flour, feed for the lowing, patient oxen and the dozen little things which found a ready sale.

He had thrived in those days, twenty years ago now and had continued to make a living until the war burst over the east. The war was three years over but trade had not revived. Somehow, though he hated to admit it, old Caleb knew that it would never revive. He stirred and shaded his eyes at a plume of dust far to the west.

'Sam!'

The sound of an axe ceased at his call.

'Sam!' The old man lifted his thin voice. 'Get over here.'

'What is it?' The undergrowth behind the store moved and a young man, dressed in old jeans, a shabby pair of boots on his feet, his head bare to the sun, stepped towards the old man. He hefted his axe as if it were part of him and, as he stared at him, old Caleb felt a quiet pride.

Sam was his grandson, the only child of his daughter who had married a hard-riding, hard-living adventurer from Texas. He had died as he had lived, in the spreading smoke of flaming guns and the young widow and child had taken the stage for Morgan's

Creek. They had never made it. A band of Indians had ambushed the stage, stolen the horses and scalped the men. The widow had died from an arrow wound and had fallen over her baby. A rescue party had found the wailing mite and delivered it to Caleb. Single-handed he had reared his grandson.

'Someone coming,' he said quietly.

'Stage?' Sam shaded his eyes and then shook his head. 'Can't be, the stage isn't due for almost a week.'

'Dust ain't high enough for the stage,' said Caleb. 'Not for a wagon either.' He shaded his eyes again. 'I'd guess a lone rider.'

'Want me to get the rifle and hide?'

'What for?' Caleb grinned at Sam's expression. 'You've learned well, Sam, though I say so myself. But the war's over and you ain't a child no more. You're full grown. There ain't no human coyotes on the prowl now and it ain't necessary for you to cover me with the rifle while I dicker with whoever's coming. Let's meet him like a couple of civilized people.'

'You think your way,' said Sam. 'I think mine. I'll get the rifle.'

He looked at the approaching plume of dust, gauged the distance, and nodded. As softly as he had come he slipped towards the store, vanished inside and came out with a Winchester. He checked the loading, smiled towards the old man and then vanished into the undergrowth. Alone, old Caleb shook his head at the precaution.

Once it had been necessary. A few years ago when Sam had been a child and the roads filled with wartorn men, prowling outlaws and trigger-happy gunmen, he had saved the store and the house from looting and burning, the old man from immediate death. Then they had arranged the system where Sam would lie hidden with his rifle, hidden and watchful, ready to shoot and kill to protect the store and his grandfather's life. Sometimes it had been necessary to fire a warning shot and once he had actually killed a man.

Caleb didn't like to think of that.

He tried to bring up the boy to be better than himself but some things could not be avoided. The middle west was in a state of turmoil, the far west the haunt of Indians. A man had to know how to shoot and hit what he aimed at. He had to assess danger, be ready to meet it and act when action was called for. So he had taught Sam how to use a rifle, taught him how to hide and watch and wait his time. It was a lesson well learned.

Caleb relaxed, warm in the knowledge of his watching protector, and waited for the cloud of dust to resolve itself.

It was a man, a tall, rangy, hard-eyed man. He rode a jaded gelding streaked and marked with the signs of long hard travel. He carried a pair of six-guns low on his thighs, a Winchester rested in a saddle-scabbard, and the worn hilt of a hunting-knife showed above his belt. His clothes were good though worn. His spurs were Spanish-style with big, sharp rowels and his saddle was Mexican. He drew rein opposite Caleb and stared down at the old man.

'You the boss, here?' He jerked his head towards the shack and store.

'That's right.' Caleb didn't move. But he looked at the visitor, noting the little points of interest, his old but keen brain assessing the lone rider.

His spurs and saddle spoke of south of the border, Texas at least or maybe New Mexico. His bronzed features told of an outdoor life, his good clothing of self-respect and money, though Caleb knew that meant little in a land where a cowpuncher would squander a month's pay on a new Stetson. His weapons weren't important aside from the fact that they showed the rider knew what he was doing. Most men rode heavily armed, not to do so would be foolish for, in the Indian Nations, a man's life depended on the fire-power in his hands and the fresh loads in his belt. Riding as they did far away from any store or military outpost, most hunters and prospectors had to carry their own equipment. With guns and plenty of ammunition they could both fight Indians and hunt game. Without they would fall to the first young brave out to make himself a coup.

The horse told its own story. It was a big deep-chested mount, but, despite the Spanish-type spurs, its flanks were unmarked save for one or two minor scratches. The rider had ridden long, had ridden hard, but had considered his horse.

'Well?' The tall man leaned forward from the saddle, his cold, ice-blue eyes hard. 'Seen enough?'

'Touchy,' said Caleb. 'Why?'

'You in the question asking business or do you sell livery service?'

'Both.' Caleb glanced down the trail. 'This is a lonely place, mister, and I'm an old man. I like company but I can do without owl-hoots.' He leaned back, knowing that, when angry, a man betrays himself. The tall stranger looked at him then smiled.

'So you've got a right to be cautious,' he said. 'You going to ask me to step down?'

'This ain't Texas,' said Caleb. 'A man's got the right to dismount if he wants to without waiting to be asked.'

'That's right.' The tall man swung a leg over the saddle and dropped to the ground. 'Sometimes a man forgets.'

'Sometimes a man can't afford to forget,' said Caleb. 'Not when someone says they own every foot of the range you might be riding on. Not when you call at cattle camps and ranch-houses. Especially not when any stranger might be a gunslinger come to take your measure.'

'You know Texas,' said the man. He stepped forward and held out his hand. 'My name's Wilson, Mike Wilson.'

'Caleb.' The old man rose and took the proffered hand. 'Pleased to meet you.'

Mike smiled, gripped the old man's hand then, with startling suddenness, pulled, twisted, and pressed himself

9

tight against Caleb. He moved so fast, so smoothly that before the old man knew it he was trapped, his arm gripped by the wrist across his body, the stranger behind him so that Caleb acted as a shield.

'All right,' gritted Mike. Caleb heard the unmistakable sound of a cocked pistol. 'Make a move and I'll let you have it through the kidneys.'

'I ain't moving,' said Caleb, and inwardly cursed himself for being a fool.

'See that you don't.' Something hard and round dug into the old man's back. 'Now tell whoever's in those bushes to come out with their hands empty and in the air.'

'In the bushes?' Caleb twisted his head to stare into the stranger's face. 'There ain't no one in there.'

'Do as I say.' The gun dug harder. 'I'm not fooling, mister. Give those orders or say your prayers.'

'You'll never get away with it.' Caleb swallowed and licked lips which had suddenly gone dry. He had seen a killer's expression before and he recognized it when he saw it. The stranger, he knew, would shoot without hesitation.

'You in the bushes,' he called. 'You heard the man. Come out with empty hands.'

Nothing happened, not a leaf stirred, Caleb, for all the effect he produced, could have shouted to an empty wilderness. He twisted his head and squinted at Mike.

'See? I told you there was no one there.'

'Keep still!' The deep, normally pleasant voice held a snarl. 'Try and uncover me again and I'll blast you.' The gun was a finger of steel pressed against the old man's ribs. 'Listen,' Mike shouted. 'The old man is light and I can carry him if I have to. He'll be easier to carry dead. Come out or I'll let him have it.'

Silence.

'All right,' said Mike. 'One thing is

for sure, we can't stand like this all day. That friend of yours is probably moving around to get a side-shot at me. We'll go into the shack.'

'What do you want?' Caleb guessed that Mike had spoken the truth. He could imagine Sam creeping through the undergrowth so as to get a clear shot at the stranger. But Caleb knew what the young man didn't, that the cocked gun held against his spine was prevented from firing only by the pressure of a thumb. If Sam fired and hit the stranger then Mike's pistol would fire. The bullet would be certain to kill the old man.

'Nothing.'

'What?'

'Nothing.' Mike grunted as he stared around him. 'It's just that I'm a cautious man. Call out your friend and let's get this nonsense over with.' His voice hardened. 'I don't have to tell you what happens if he cuts loose. Maybe he'll kill me, and maybe not, but you're certain to die.'

'Yes.' Caleb swallowed and lifted his voice. 'It's all right, Sam. Come on out with your hands empty.'

Silence.

'Come out, you young fool!' yelled Caleb. 'He's got his thumb on the hammer and the trigger down. Shoot and he'll kill me. Come out, Sam, everything's all right.'

Undergrowth rustled and Sam stepped into the clearing before the buildings. His hands were empty and he held them shoulder high. His young face was taut, scared but determined and Caleb knew that the fear was for him, not for Sam himself.

'Come closer.' Mike waited until the young man was well away from the bushes. 'That's better. Any more of you?'

'No.'

'You sure of that?'

'I'm telling you the truth.' Sam stepped forward. 'Let him go.'

'Why not?' Mike released the old man, stepped back, slowly uncocked his pistol. He smiled at the pair as he slipped it into his holster. 'All right, now you can get your gun if you want to.'

Sam glanced at Caleb, then at Mike.

'You heard what I said.' Mike smiled even wider. 'I'm no outlaw but I don't like walking into a trap. I figgered you for a gunslinger and the set-up here a trap. The old man makes perfect bait. You can see how it would work.'

'It wasn't that way at all.' said Caleb mildly. He looked at Sam. 'Get your rifle and meet us in the shack.'

'How would it work?' asked Sam. He was curious.

'The old man sits in the sun waiting for a victim. They talk. You cut loose from the undergrowth and the victim falls with a hole in his head. You take his horse, his clothes, guns and what's in his saddle-bags. You bury the body and don't know nothing from nothing. If the rider is a stranger no one will ask questions and you can live easy.' Mike jerked out the sentences as if impatient

14

at having to explain.

'Would people do things like that?' Sam frowned as he thought about it.

'They would, and do,' said Mike grimly. He turned to his horse. 'Can you put up my mount? Feed, water, and rub down. I want the best.'

'You'll get the best,' said Caleb.

'Maybe. Walk it around for a spell before giving water. Oats if you have any.'

'Sam'll take care of it.' Caleb took Mike's arm. 'Let's go inside.'

Mike nodded but, at the entrance to the shack, paused and stared about him. He stared for a long time towards the west, scanning the far horizon and, when he finally ducked inside the clapboard cabin, his face was thoughtful. He became more thoughtful when Sam reported on the state of the horse.

'It's all in,' said the youngster. 'You've ridden it to the limit and it's strained a fetlock. It'll have to rest.'

'Have you other horses?'

'No.'

'No?' Mike looked surprised. 'How's that?'

'One of the stage coaches had a smash,' explained the young man. 'They lost four horses and took all we had. They'll replace them next time — but that won't be for almost a week.'

'A week!' The tall man stared towards the window. Outside it was growing dark, the sun sinking towards the west, painting the rolling prairie with long fingers of red and orange so that the swollen ball of the sun seemed to be sinking into a sea of blood.

'You can stay here while you wait,' said Caleb. 'We've got extra beds and plenty of food.' He smiled. 'We'll be glad of the company.'

'Thanks,' said Mike absently. 'Does all traffic this way come along the trail?'

'The little that does come.' said Caleb. 'Why?'

'No reason.' Mike looked at Sam. 'How soon will my horse be fit to travel?'

'Two days, maybe three. You'll have

to take it easy, though.'

'Any other horses around? I can pay top prices for one.'

'The nearest place is Morgan's Landing, about twenty miles north of here.' said Sam. 'I guess that a man could make it in a couple of days, buy a horse and get back here by the third day.'

'Two days for twenty miles?'

'It's rough country,' explained Caleb. 'It's over the hills most of the way. That twenty miles I talked about was the shortest route. On the trail it's nearer thirty.'

Caleb set a bottle and glasses on the rough, plank table. Set out tin plates, a loaf of bread, a big pan of bacon and beans. A smoke-blackened pot redolent of coffee hung over the fire and the old man filled three tin cups from it. He drew a stool up to the table. 'Sit and eat,' he ordered. 'Before it gets cold.'

The food was rough, camp fare but the stranger ate like a man who has lived on the edge of starvation too long.

He emptied his plate, refilled it, emptied it and then scraped the bottom of the pot. He sat back, took a slender cigar from his pocket, lit it and breathed smoke.

'Like a drink?' Caleb filled two glasses from the bottle. 'Good stuff though I say it myself.' He grinned. 'No label though.'

'Corn squeezings?' Mike sipped at the potent spirit, nodded, swallowed a mouthful. 'I've drunk a lot worse from fancy bottles with fancy names.'

'In the war?' asked Caleb slyly. He was curious with the curiosity of the aged. The tall stranger presented a problem. He spoke like a gentleman, the idiom and roughness of the west overlaid a more cultured tone. He acted like a man very sure of himself and yet, about him, was an aura of the hunted. His equipment was good, he spoke casually of money, and yet he ate like a man who was a stranger to food.

'Maybe.'

'Were you in the war?' Sam, all

attention, stared at the tall man. To a boy reared in almost complete isolation Mike represented a breath of the outside world about which he had only heard rumours. Grown as Sam was in a physical sense, taught as he had been by his grandfather, yet, in many ways, he was innocent and ignorant of life. 'Did you see any fighting?'

'Too much.' Mike hesitated, looking at the thin thread of smoke from his cigar. 'Four years of it, Sam, four years of misery. War is bad but when brother fights brother it is hell. I've seen — ' He shook his head. 'Never mind that now. It's over, all over and best forgotten.'

'They say that the North went to war to end slavery,' said Caleb thoughtfully. 'It's always struck me as bad that men should own other men and work them like animals. The colour of the skin don't make no difference when it comes to that.'

'Slavery was just a part of the question,' said Mike.

'The main part of it, I'd say,' insisted

Caleb. 'Seems to me that a man who owns slaves ain't no better than he should be.'

'You're entitled to your opinion,' said Mike. He drew at his cigar. 'I take it that your sympathies were with the Union?'

'I ain't got no sympathies,' said Caleb. 'I came out west when we was still using flintlocks and the Ohio was the frontier. It seems to me kind of silly to squabble when there's all this land waiting for the taking. Seems there's no call for slaves or fighting over owning men and women, not when a man can ride for a week and see nothing but prairie and buffalo.'

'What about the Indians? If they're fighting to hold what they claim is theirs then they must reckon on owning the land.'

'Sure, but that's their hard luck.' Caleb helped himself to more home-made whiskey. 'If they ain't strong enough to hold what they claim is theirs then they must reckon to lose it. White men have got to live somewhere.'

'About this slavery,' said Sam; he frowned as he thought about it. 'Did you ever own slaves?'

'Maybe.'

'That would make you a Southerner, wouldn't it?'

'Maybe.' Mike looked again at his cigar. 'But not all who fought for the Confederation were born in the South. Texas was a part of the Confederacy, remember, and there were a lot of sympathizers in Oregon and California.' He stared at his cigar and seemed to come to a decision. 'Look Sam, you've probably heard a lot of false talk from people who don't know better. The war wasn't just fought over the slave question, never think that. It was fought because a lot of people didn't like the idea of being told what to do by a lot of other people. Slavery was one thing the North pledged itself to end.'

'And a good thing too,' said Sam hotly.

'Was it?' Mike shrugged. 'You haven't

seen the South, I have. I remember it as it was before the war and I've seen it after. Once there was big plantations and good houses. We had a nice society growing cotton, making things, living our own life in our own way. There were slaves, yes, and there were masters who treated their slaves like dirt. I can't defend that. But look at it now.'

'You're a Southerner,' said Caleb triumphantly. 'And I bet that you were an officer. Right.'

'Right. I was a Major.'

'I knew it,' said the old man, and chuckled at having solved his private problem. Mike stared, knowing that he could take offence if he wished, but knowing too that the old man was harmless in his little deceptions. He smiled at Sam.

'Kinfolk?'

'My grandfather, he raised me since I was born.'

'Did he teach you to hide out with a rifle?'

'Yes,' Sam stared at Mike as if

troubled by a sudden thought. 'I meant to ask you about that. How did you know I was there?'

'I saw a bird rise and fly away. I saw another circle for a landing then change its mind. I saw a leaf move when there was no wind.' Mike shrugged.

'Is that all?'

'That and a sense that something was wrong. I learnt it before and during the war. I could always tell when the enemy were near, just a guess I suppose you'd call it, but it saved my neck more than once.'

'You was talking about the war,' said Caleb, he was impatient for Mike to get talking again. Life at the store was a lonely thing and fresh talk was, to the old man, prime entertainment.

'Yes,' said Mike, and sat, thoughtful, his cold blue eyes misted as he stared down the paths of memory. 'The North won and Sherman marched to the sea. You've heard of Sherman? He burned Atlanta and ravaged the heart of the South. He destroyed, wantonly, deliberately, tearing the economic guts out of the country so that they could never recover to fight again. And, naturally, the slaves were freed.'

'Good,' said Sam.

'Good, for whom?' Mike sighed and smoked for a while in silence. 'The slaves were freed — to starve. The masters were dead or dispossessed. The fields are lying idle and there's very little food. Slaves are wandering all over the South together with discharged soldiers, dispossessed civilians, the sweep and rabble of war. The Union said they would treat the negroes as equals, which meant nothing but they gave them the right to vote, and sent in the carpet baggers to gain those votes for their own people.'

'And you?'

'I went home to ruin. My family all dead, my home burned, my land stolen for non-payment of taxes I knew nothing about. I had a horse, a little money, and no home. So I rode across the border, headed west, made what I could where I could.' Mike crushed out the butt of his cigar. 'I don't like to talk about it.'

'But — ' Sam was insistent.

'I said that I didn't want to talk about it!' For a moment Mike's face wore the same expression old Caleb had seen before. Hard, cold, ruthless, the face of an impatient killer. Sam swallowed, abashed, and yet, with the burning eagerness of youth, determined to learn all he could.

Caleb had other ideas.

'Fill 'em up,' he said, and tilted the bottle over the empty glasses. 'How about you, Sam, you reckon you could take a drink without keeling over?'

'I don't know.' Never before had the old man offered him spirits. Mike looked from one to the other.

'He don't drink?'

'No.'

'Then why make him?' Mike sipped on his own whiskey. Caleb stared at the tall man, his eyes shrewd.

'You've been around, Mike,' he said.

'So have I. Sam here, ain't, and I reckon that I'm to blame. I've tried to wet-nurse him, brought him up straight and true but an old man ain't company for a young one.' He took a mouthful of whiskey. 'How many men do you know, Mike, who don't drink?'

'A few.' Mike stared at his glass. 'Wyatt Earp for one. He don't drink. Sam Levin for another, he don't drink either.'

'Two out of how many?' Caleb shrugged. 'Go anywhere in the west and you'll find bars and taverns. There ain't no other place for men to meet. A non-drinker gets himself known, gets gunslingers aiming to have fun at his expense. All right, so Earp and Levin don't drink, but they had to buy the right to step into a saloon and not be laughed at the hard way. Am I right?'

'So?'

'So Sam should learn how to hold his liquor. If he don't like it he can leave it alone. But I'd be a poor teacher not to show him what he's got to face.' The old man stared at Mike, hoping for his approval. Instead the tall man shrugged and, as before, his eyes strayed to the window.

It was late twilight now, the sun below the horizon and the first dimness of night creeping over the sky. From the house the trail wound like a painted stripe over the nutbrown ground. twisting as it led down to the tiny spring known as Morgan's Creek.

It was quiet, deathly quiet, even the jays having ceased their chatter and gone to roost. From somewhere, a long way off, the howl of a coyote echoed like the cry of a lost soul. It broke off, was repeated, then the howl was taken up from closer at hand.

'Coyotes,' said Caleb. 'Never known 'em come so near before.'

'They ain't coyotes,' said Mike quietly.

'No?' Caleb listened to the distant howling. 'What are they then?'

'Indians!'

The howling came nearer.

2

'Indians, eh?' Caleb squinted from the window. 'We ain't had Indians around here for five years now. Used to be a tribe of Sioux hanging around after tobacco and sugar, whiskey too when they could get it, but they was pushed back into the Nations after the treaty.'

Mike stared from the window. 'I was afraid of this. There's trouble all through Indian Territory and talk of breaking out and going on the warpath. Some of the young chiefs are eager to collect a few coup, get some scalps so that they can strut before the squaws. Red Arrow is trying to hold them back but most won't listen!'

'How do you know?' said Caleb.

'I've just ridden through the Indian Country.' Wilson shrugged at the old man's expression. 'I guessed that they were trailing me but I wasn't sure.'

'Why should they do that?' Caleb shifted nervously on his stool. He had vivid memories of other Indian uprisings, the scalping, the attacks, the burnings, the violent deaths and the screaming, yelling, blood-crazed Indians, painted and feathered like devils.

'I was official hunter with a party of surveyors,' said Mike calmly. 'They were plotting the route for the new railroad heading through Kansas. I was out on a hunt and while I was away, they attacked the party. I heard the shots and circled back. I arrived just in time to run into a party of warriors.'

'And the others?' Sam asked.

'Dead, I guess,' said Mike evenly. 'I didn't stay to find out. I emptied my six-guns at the Indians and rode away at top speed. After a while they gave up the chase but all the way here I've had the feeling that I've been watched.'

'You didn't stay to help them!' Sam was shocked. 'But supposing some of them had still been alive? You could have rescued them. You mean to say that you just rode away?'

'That's right.' Mike stared at the young man, his eyes cold. 'Now call me a coward.'

'Don't do it!' Caleb jumped up and stood between the two men. 'He's young, Mike, and don't know what he's saying.' He turned to his grandson. 'Watch your tongue, you young fool!'

'I know he rode off and left his friends to the mercy of the Indians,' said Sam sullenly. 'He said so.'

'What else could he have done?' Caleb was angry with rage induced by fear. 'Stayed and got himself scalped or maybe worse? Have you ever seen what the Indians do to a prisoner? No, of course you haven't, but until you do never think a man scared because he thinks of his own hide.'

'That's not the way I see it.' said Sam. 'How can we hope to beat the Indians unless we stick together?'

'Listen,' said Mike. He gestured Caleb to silence. 'I told you I rode in at the finish. All right, now let's not talk about that. Let's talk about what could have happened to me instead. I've fought Indians before the war and I've seen what they do. If I told you some of their tortures you'd be sick or you wouldn't believe me. But your grand-father knows and you'd believe him. They would have taken me and put me to death. Then, because of having wiped out the entire party, they would have gone on the warpath.'

'Weren't they on it already?'

'No. The surveying party ran up against a bunch of young braves.' Mike shrugged. 'They were on the warpath, right enough, but it was a private thing, not a full-scale uprising. They went against the orders of Red Arrow in putting on warpaint and going out to collect coup, but that isn't important. The important thing is that I'm the only survivor. If they wipe me out then no one need know what happened to the surveying party. If I get through I'll report the massacre to General Clarke at Fort Hemridge.'

'What can he do?'

'Send out cavalry to warn Red Arrow. Maybe burn a couple of villages and show the Indians what to expect if they try any tricks.'

'Warn Red Arrow!' Sam looked disgusted. 'Why doesn't he just ride in and settle things?'

Sam, despite the best education Caleb could give him, still lacked a great deal of understanding. To him, as to most youngsters, things were simple. The Indians were troublesome — kill them. The South had slavery — so war against the South to stop it.

'Indians are people, Sam,' said Mike. 'Just like you and me. Their skins aren't the same colour and they think differently to us, but they are men and women, babies and children just like any other race. They've lived here far longer than we have, and they think that the ground they hunt on, and their fathers hunted on before them, is theirs. Can you blame them for that?'

'No,' admitted Sam. 'But all this

scalping and burning, only animals or beasts would do that.'

'I told you that they think differently from us,' said Mike. 'And what about us? We've taken the land from the Indians and then think we've done wonders in giving them a little of it back as a reservation. The Indian Territory is Indian Land, we gave it to them. Yet we keep stealing it back. Our word isn't to be trusted as far as an Indian is concerned.'

'All right,' said Sam. He preferred to think of it as he always had, that Indians were bad and that the only good Indian was a dead one. 'But what of this latest uprising?'

'It isn't an uprising, no more than it would be a war if you tried to rob a bank and killed someone doing it. Never forget that, as far as the Indians are concerned, that surveying party shouldn't have been where they were. They were trespassers and ran the risk of being attacked. They were attacked and wiped out. That's all there is to it.'

'Is it?' Caleb listened at the windows. What about those coyote cries outside?'

'They're after me,' said Mike. 'They've been trailing me for a week now and I haven't dared sleep in all that time.'

'You led them to us,' said Sam. 'They'll attack us!'

'They probably will,' agreed Mike. He felt for a fresh cigar, lit it, blew smoke towards the window. 'I wasn't sure that they were after me until I heard their signals. Now we're all in trouble. I would have ridden out with you, but you have no horses. Like it or not we've got to stay here.'

'Sitting pigeons,' said Sam, bitterly. He glanced towards his grandfather. 'Three men against how many Indians?'

'Maybe a couple of dozen,' said Mike. 'Maybe less.'

'Nothing to it,' snorted Caleb. 'Two men and a boy ought to be enough to tackle that lot.'

'Three men,' corrected Mike. 'Sam's full-grown.'

'Thanks,' said Sam. He became thoughtful. 'What shall we do?'

'Fight,' said Mike simply. 'How many guns have you got?'

'My Winchester,' said Sam. 'A shotgun and a .45.'

'More than that,' said Caleb. 'There are a dozen pistols in the store, a half-dozen shotguns and as many rifles with ammunition to boot.' He chuckled. 'Sam forgets that we can use the stock if we want to.'

'Good.' Mike examined the walls of the cabin. They were too thin to stop a bullet, though they would give some protection against arrows. He shook his head. 'Are the walls of the store thicker than the cabin?'

'Sure. I built the store first and I built it strong. That was back in the days of the Sioux raids on the settlements. I built it of solid logs and fitted loopholes. The timber's weathered a little and it ain't as strong as it used to be but it's better than this.'

'We'll shift over there.' Mike rose and

picked up the whiskey bottle. 'Bring what you need, everything you need, and let's get going.'

The store, as Caleb had claimed, was still strong. Mike lit a lantern, examined the structure, and frowned as he noticed the absolute dryness of the store. With little rain and plenty of sun the timbers had dried out. He said nothing, merely checked the loopholes, saw that they covered the immediate ground, then turned to where Caleb was busy.

'Any water close to here?'

'A creek back of the house. Why?'

'We'd better get some, Sam. Fill all the buckets you can find and bring them in here. Where's the stable?'

'Back in the underbrush.'

'That's all right.' Mike waited until the young man had left on his errand and then turned to Caleb. The old man was loading his store of firearms, taking cartridges from waxed paper boxes and filling the chambers of the revolvers and the magazines of the rifles. Mike picked up a shotgun and reached for loads.

'Buckshot?'

'That's right, nine to the load.'

Mike nodded, then tensed as a coyote howled from outside. Taking the shotgun he blew out the lantern, and siipped from the store. It was quite dark by this time, the cabin a hulking shadow and the underbrush a mass of deeper darkness. Though it was night the stars shone in the sky and a quarter moon had risen. In the moon and starlight details slowly became visible. Mike dropped to one knee as a shadow moved towards him.

'Sam?'

'Yes.' Sam started as the tall man arose from the ground before him. 'Anything wrong?'

'No. Take that water inside and stay there.'

'Where are you going?'

'To the stable. I want my saddle, rifle and saddle-bags.'

'They're in the store,' said Sam. 'I took them there when I bedded down the horse. In the corner by the door.'

'I didn't see them.' Mike didn't look at Sam as he spoke, he stared towards the undergrowth and kept his voice low.

'I put a blanket over them,' explained Sam.' He stared behind him. 'Are they close?'

'I don't know.' Mike jerked his head. 'Get that water inside and grab a gun. Don't shoot me by mistake.'

'Aren't you coming with me?'

'No. I'm going to take a scout. I'll whistle when I return and you open the door fast.' The tall man chuckled. 'I might be in a hurry.'

Sam hesitated for a moment and then, hefting his water buckets, moved towards the store. Mike stared after him, smiling to himself. Sam could be no more than sixteen yet, here on the frontier, he was accounted a grown man. He could fight, kill, die if he had to the same as any man born. In the West responsibility, when it came, came fast and heavy. Boys became men almost overnight and age had little to do with it.

He felt no regret that he had led the Indians to the old man and his grandson. It was just one of those things like his being away when the surveying party had been wiped out. He felt no regret about that either, he had run away because to remain would have been a foolish waste of his life. His message, while not that important, could help to remind the Indians that the arm of the white man was long. Unless he got through then Red Arrow would know nothing of the action of his braves or, if he knew, could do nothing about it. Even if he didn't deliver the message Mike knew that he wouldn't worry about it. He had seen too much of death.

Now he had his own skin to think of and he concentrated on the scout. He dropped and immediately vanished in the undergrowth. He moved forward, silently, and yet he knew not as silently as an Indian. Carrying a shotgun under one arm he stole forward towards where a coyote had howled only a few moments before. It howled again, then again, and yet a third time. Mike tensed, crouching on the ground, his eyes narrowed as they peered into the starlit darkness.

A shadow moved before him.

It was a shadow, nothing more, yet it moved, stood upright, and, as it passed, left the rancid smell of grease on the air. Mike sniffed it, recognizing it for what it was, the invariable scent of an Indian caused by their habit of rubbing grease on their bodies. He waited as a second shadow drifted past, a third, then, for a long time, waited without doing any more than to breathe. No other shadows passed and he rose, continuing his forward motion in the direction the Indians had gone. He halted just in time.

Three Indians sat around a small fire and conversed in guttural Sioux. The fire was shade, smokeless and, in the still air, scentless from a few feet away. Some horses stood a little away from the fire and Mike counted them. Fifteen of the wiry, saddleless ponies were tethered together which meant that a dozen Indians were surrounding the store and cabin. An Indian muttered something and reached forward to the fire. A chip of wood fell and threw a momentary light into his face.

It was a devil's mask. One half was painted a dead black, the other a brilliant red. Yellow ringed the eyes and mouth and wavy lines of the same colour ran across the forehead. The Indian lifted his head and stared directly towards where Mike was lying. Even as the glow from the fire died the tall man was on his feet, the shotgun thrown forward and his finger tightening on the trigger.

The blast of a shotgun sent echoes rumbling from the hills and painted the scene with a vivid gash of flame. Eighteen heavy buckshot, the full load of both barrels, slammed towards the painted warrior and the side of his face painted black ran sudden crimson. He fell without a word, crashing down on to the tiny fire, his blood extinguishing the red embers.

As he fell Mike dropped the shotgun, snatched out his Colts and rolled the hammers with experienced thumbs. He fired left-right-left, alternating each gun as he sent lead blasting towards the other two Indians. The light was bad, the targets were dim, but instinct and firepower gave him the advantage. A warrior screamed as death clawed at him, tried to throw his tomahawk and died as it left his hand. The second Indian turned, then crashed through the undergrowth as lead smashed his spine.

It was slaughter, cold, calculated, efficient, but Mike didn't think of that. He had fired first and without warning because he had wanted to kill the Indians without being killed. Their paint had warned him and directed his actions. The paint was warpaint, the Indian warriors on the warpath, and it had been his life or theirs.

His and Caleb's and Sam's.

3

Sam opened the door at Mike's whistle and the tall man slipped into the store. He slammed the door behind him, stepped over to the lantern and opened the side-gate of his right-hand Colt. Deftly he extracted the used cartridges, took fresh loads from his belt and filled the empty chambers. He did the same with the left-hand gun, eased both weapons in their holsters and glanced at the guns on the long wooden counter.

'Everything loaded to the full?'

'Yes.' Caleb looked worried. 'I heard the firing. Trouble?'

'I got three of them,' said Mike. 'I lost the shotgun but you can find it again if we live through this. There are at least a dozen Indians in warpaint after our blood. They wanted it before but they will be crazy for it now that

44

I've killed three of their number in the dark.'

'Does that make any difference?' Sam was at a loophole, his Winchester in his hands. He turned as he asked the question.

'Indians don't like dying at night,' said Mike. 'They think that their spirits can't see the way to the Happy Hunting Grounds. They'll only attack in the dark if desperate or mad with rage.' He blew out the lantern. 'Those redskins out there are mad with rage. Fire until you can't fire any more but remember one thing.'

'What?' Sam squinted through his loophole. 'What's the one thing?'

'Use the last bullet on yourself,' said Mike grimly. He tensed as a yelling war whoop came from outside. 'Here they come!'

They came in a rush, shooting, yelling, screaming their heads off as they charged against the store. Fire met them, stabs of flames from the loopholes and, when they retired, three twisted shapes writhed on the ground.

'Nine to go,' said Mike. 'If they keep this up it'll be a walk-over.'

'You think they will?' Caleb was worried about Sam and he couldn't hide his fear that the boy would be killed or hurt. His eagerness to be comforted was pathetic.

'No.' Mike levelled his rifle and fired at a shadow. 'I think that they'll fire the cabin and stable to get light. Then, unless they're plain stupid, they'll fire this store.' He touched the woodwork. 'If they do we'll have to leave here shooting. This place is a fire-trap.'

'There's a sky-light I built into the roof,' said Caleb. 'I used to have a little watch-tower up there. I could climb up with some water and douse the fire arrows as they come.'

'You stay down here.' Mike fired again then grunted as a wash of red came from the undergrowth. 'There goes the stable.' He fired again, swore, levered a fresh cartridge into the chamber and fired again. A yell answered the shot.

'Dead?'

'Winged him.' Mike scowled at the old man. 'Get a gun and find a loophole, keep firing and quit hanging around my shoulder.'

Caleb nodded and did as he was told. For a few minutes the interior of the store echoed with the blast of guns as the defenders aimed at dancing shapes illuminated by the burning stable. Mike aimed and fired with a cold mastery of his weapon. Caleb with a kind of desperation, sending his shots into the night, his old eyes unable to take a correct sight. Sam was good but shooting screaming Indians was different to his normal target practice. Even at that he wounded a couple, smashing the leg of one and hitting another in the side.

By the time the second charge had retreated three more bodies lay on the ground.

'That makes nine dead,' said Mike. 'If my count was right there are six

Indians out there, maybe some of them wounded.' He stepped to a bucket and drank deeply of the spring water. 'Caleb, you load. Sam, forget your target practice and don't hang on the bead too long. Just keep firing fast and smooth. An Indian's a big target and it doesn't matter where you hit him. The point is that, while you're shooting at him, he can't concentrate on shooting at you.' Mike grinned at the youngster. 'Don't worry about how many shells you're using, we've plenty of ammunition.'

Ruby light shone through the loopholes and a roaring gush of flame lined the clearing with brilliant light. The cabin, its clapboards as dry as tinder, had been fired by the Indians and the area outside the store was now as light as day. From the undergrowth came an erratic firing and the sharp, wicked hum of arrows lanced towards the defenders.

'Watch for fire arrows,' warned Mike. 'Spot any gleam of flame and fire at it.' He grunted as his rifle misfired, a shell had stuck in the heat-expanded breech. He jerked the lever, swore, threw aside the weapon and took another from the counter.

Sam cried out in sudden pain and reeled back from the loophole. Caleb, his face white, darted towards the youngster.

'Sam! Where did they get you?'

'Back to your post!' Mike snarled as he grabbed the old man by the shoulder. 'Back!'

'Sam's hurt!' Caleb pulled himself free from the tall man and sprang to the boy's side. 'Sam! Sam!'

'Get back!' Mike jerked the old man away, thrust a rifle into his hands, flung him towards a loophole. 'Damn it, they'll be on us in a moment.'

'But Sam — '

'Forget Sam!' Mike trained his rifle through a loophole and sent a stream of lead towards a spot in the undergrowth where little fires leapt and danced. He thinned his lips as arrows, each bound with a grease-soaked rag, each flaming as they drove through the air, lanced towards the roof of the store. They landed and the tall man could guess what was happening to the tinder-dry structure. Bitterly he fired at a point of fire, heard a scream then fired again as a painted warrior toppled from cover. The brave jerked as lead smashed into his body then lay still. A second Indian, his face grotesque in the firelight, darted towards the dead man, paused, hurled his tomahawk at the building, and died as bullets tore into his painted body.

'Four.' said Mike. 'Only four left. When are they going to run?'

He scowled through the loophole at the undergrowth, saw no signs of life, then turned to see how badly the youngster was hurt. He found him leaning over a bucket, the water stained red with his blood.

'Where did they hit you?'

'In the head.' Sam splashed water on his forehead.

'Let me see.' Mike tilted the boy's

head and stared at the wound. It was a long, shallow gash just above the ear on the left-hand side of the head. A bullet had creased the youngster, stunning him with the shock but doing little more than tear the skin.

'How bad is it?' Caleb left his post and stared at Sam.

'Just a flesh wound.' Mike stared about the store. 'Where's the whiskey?'

'You want a drink?' Caleb didn't move.

'I want the whiskey.' Mike grabbed at a bottle, drew the cork, sniffed the contents and flung the bottle aside. 'Gun oil. Where's the whiskey?'

'Here.' Caleb, half-afraid of the tall man, extended the bottle. Mike grabbed it smelt it, tasted it, and nodded.

'This is going to hurt, Sam,' he warned. 'It's going to hurt like hell, but it'll stop the bleeding and prevent infection.' He gripped the youngster's hair, twisted his head so that the wound was uppermost and poised the bottle.

'Close your eyes.'

'What?'

'Close your eyes!' Mike waited until the boy had squeezed shut his eyes then, deliberately, he poured the raw spirit into the open wound.

Sam screamed.

He shrieked like an injured horse, twisted, then slumped into unconsciousness. Quickly, before he could recover, Mike swabbed the wound with more whiskey.

'Got to do it,' he said. 'Them Indians have a habit of leaving their bullets in rotten meat and other stuff. This will prevent infection.' He finished his crude doctoring, took a drink of whiskey and handed the bottle to the old man.

'Take a drink,' he ordered. 'You look worse than Sam. Give him a drink when he comes to.'

'Where are you going?' Caleb looked up as the tall man sprang to his feet.

'They've set fire to the roof. Can't you smell it?' He sniffed and his nostrils wrinkled to the odour of burning wood.

The temperature inside the store had risen so that the sweat glistened in great beads on their foreheads. Minutes would see the collapse of the roof and total destruction for all inside.

'Wake Sam up,' said Mike. 'Slap him, anything, but get him on his feet.' He snatched up a rifle and went to a loophole. He was lucky. An Indian, emboldened by the silence from the burning store, had left his cover and was running forward. Mike shot him, sent more lead towards the bushes, then stared thoughtfully towards the door.

'How's Sam?'

'I'm all right.' The youngster staggered to his feet. 'What did you do to me?'

'Forget it, it's over.' Mike stared up at the roof. It was glowing dull red and sparks were cascading down from the burning timbers. 'Listen, we've got to get out of here. As far as I see it there are only three Indians outside. I just shot one while he was running towards the building. My guess is that the others are waiting just outside. They know we can't stay in here and, when we break free, they'll cut us down.' He thinned his lips. 'Unless we cut them down first.'

'Can we?' Caleb looked doubtful.

'We might. Here's what we do. You and Sam take a pair of Colts each and a shotgun apiece. I'll do the same. We open the door and run outside. You fire towards the left and I'll attend to the right. If those Indians are waiting for us then we're bound to get them. Right?'

Caleb nodded and Mike passed them the weapons.

'Shoot often, shoot fast, shoot to kill. Ready?'

They nodded.

'Right!' Mike dropped the bar, dragged open the door and jumped outside. Even as he moved his shot-gun twisted sideways and, even before he had left shelter, he had jerked the triggers. Both barrels roared and a hail of buckshot blasted along the side of the building. Nothing human could have lived through such a hail and nothing did. A red warrior, his head a smashed ruin, toppled forward from where he had sat, rifle ready, to kill the escaping white men.

A second shotgun roared, then a third as Sam and Caleb repeated Mike's manoeuvre. Then the three were out of the burning store and racing for the undergrowth.

'Did you get any?' Mike had dropped the shotgun and his Colts glistened red in his hands as the fire-light was reflected from the long barrels.

'One.' Sam paused to allow Caleb to catch up with him.

'One?' Mike looked at the young man. 'But you fired twice?'

'At the same Indian,' confessed Sam. 'Grandpa only winged him and I had to finish the job.'

'That means there's still one alive somewhere.' Mike stared at the cover before him. 'Hell!'

'Maybe he's rode off?' suggested Sam. 'He must know that he doesn't stand a chance against the three of us.'

'Doesn't he?' Mike grabbed Caleb and ran towards the undergrowth. 'With him in cover and us silhouetted against the fight? Even an Indian could pick us off one at a time if he had a repeating rifle.'

'Maybe we killed one more than we thought.' said Sam. 'Maybe one of those we wounded rode away from the light?'

'Maybe.'

'Take it easy,' gasped Caleb. 'I ain't so young as I used to be and can't run so good no more. Take it easy.' He slowed, gasping, then stopped and stared back at the burning store. 'Twenty years,' he said. 'Twenty years I've lived in those buildings. I built them myself with my own two hands and — '

He gave a soft grunt, a wheezing sigh then, slowly falling as if all the strength and life had poured out of him, he sank to the ground. From the side of his neck, the gaudy feathers stained by firelight, the shaft of an arrow pointed towards the sky.

'Grandpa!' Sam caught the old man as he fell.

'They got me.' Caleb stared up with dying eyes. 'The varmints got me.'

He started to the rolling thunder of Colts.

'That's the last one,' said Mike grimly. 'I spotted him and sent him on his way. That's one warrior who won't be collecting any more scalps.' He stooped over the old man, his face softening. 'How is it, old timer?'

'I'm cashing in,' said Caleb. His thin hand gripped Mike's arm. 'Sam,' he gasped. 'Take care of Sam.'

'Sure,' said Mike gently. 'I'll take care of him.'

Caleb smiled, tried to speak, then coughed a gout of blood. Limply he relaxed, his eyes staring up at the flame-lit sky, the sky which had lasted for an eternity and would go on and on while men like him, the tough old pioneers who had tamed a wilderness, died in the dirt which had given them birth.

'He's dead,' said Sam. He didn't seem able to believe it.

'He's dead.' Mike knelt beside the silent figure of the old man. Gently he closed the staring eyes and folded the thin hands across the chest. Taking his bowie from his belt he cut the arrow close to the skin and threw away the shaft. He rose and looked around him. 'Better find a spot to bury him. Know of one?'

'They killed him.' Sam seemed dazed with the shock of seeing his grandfather, the man who had acted as both parents, lying in his own blood on the ground.

'It was them or him,' said Mike. 'We lost one man, they lost fifteen.'

'They shot him down like a dog.' Sam swallowed and bit his lips. 'A nice old man who never did any harm to anyone and they've burned his home and killed him.'

'It's life,' said Mike. He looked

58

around at the clearing. The store was now well alight, the walls awash with flame. Sharp explosions from the raging inferno told of detonating cartridges. In the firelight the sprawled bodies of the dead Indians looked like rag dolls tossed down by some wanton child.

Mike shrugged; it was, as he had said, life. Men killed and were killed, they died or they lived, they built or they destroyed. To him the death of the old man and the burning of the store was but an incident in a period holding too many such incidents. He had seen bigger burnings, more dead, had lost those closer to him than the old man could ever be.

'Where shall we bury him?' He reached out and shook the youngster. 'Snap out of it, Sam! We've got work to do.'

'Yes,' Sam drew in a deep breath. 'There's a spot just by the creek, he'd have chosen it himself.' He clenched his hands, torn between tears and rage. 'I'll get them for this,' he said brokenly.

'I'll get them if I have to kill every damn Injun in the country. You'll see.'

'They're already dead.' said Mike. He had heard such vengeance-oaths before and knew that sanity could return after the shock had faded. 'Let's get him buried, shall we?'

He stooped and picked up the body.

4

Red Arrow, Chief of the Sioux, stood before his tepee and stared over the village of his people. He was a tall man, his high, feathered headdress making him seem taller than he was. His face had sunken through age and his body was all muscle and sinew without a trace of fat. His nose thrust forward like the beak of an eagle and his eyes, deep-set and surrounded with wrinkles, were as clear as those of a younger man.

He wore a beaded tunic of buckskins tanned and gnawed by the squaws until it was soft and supple as silk. His trousers were of buffalo hide, thick and capable of withstanding hard wear. They, like his tunic, were fringed and ornamented with beadwork. Moccasins were on his feet, a long sash around his waist, and his headdress, filled with feathers, hung down almost to the ground. At his waist he carried tomahawk and knife but bore no other weapons. So he stood, the Great Chief of the Sioux, the plains Indians who ruled the middle west from Canada to Arizona, the buffalo-hunting peoples who had roamed the wide prairies long before the white man had come from beyond the sea.

But Red Arrow was troubled.

He had fought hard against the Cheyenne, the Comanche, the Apache and the Shoshone of the far west. He had ridden at the head of his young men, as befitted a chief, against the long wagon trains of the settlers. He had fought the Long Knives, the cavalry, and had waged war against hunters and trappers who robbed the Indian of their game. He had fought long and well for many years, negotiating treaty after treaty, seeing the white man break his word again and again, and yet striving for the peace he knew was so essential to his people.

Now he was old, his blood thick in his veins. Younger men spoke of him around the camp fires as one who once great, was great no longer. Now, at this time, he knew that he alone could hold the scattered tribes of the Sioux and use them as an edged tool against the invaders. But he had seen much of war and much of life. He had seen the white men and their soldiers and knew, deep within himself, that the sands of the Indians were running out.

And now the shining metal rails of the railroad were driving through the heart of the lands given to the Indians by the white men.

Once again they had broken their word, turned their treaty into valueless paper, and once again the red man had to fight or accept degradation and the loss of all he held to be his.

Red Arrow sighed then turned as a rider, crouched low over the neck of his pony, thundered towards the village. It was Bent Feather, a young warrior who had barely taken his first scalp. He tugged at his reins, slipped from his mount and ran towards Red Arrow.

'The white men are building forward,' he gasped. His bare torso glistened with perspiration. 'For many days I have watched their camps to see what they would do. Today the Long Knives arrived at the camp and work commenced at once. Many men and many guns have come from the east.'

'It is well.' Red Arrow glanced up towards the sun. 'The Council will meet when the sun has lowered itself towards the horizon a hand-span from now. Rest and eat and be ready to tell your story.'

Bent Feather nodded. He led his pony towards the edge of the village and handed the reins to his young son, Little Cloud. The boy took the pony and removed the halter of rawhide before sending it into the rough corral to feed with the other mounts. Without a backward glance Bent Feather walked to his tepee where his squaw waited, working on an elaborate tunic ornamented with bead-work and feathers for her eldest son's use after his initiation. She stared at her husband, put aside the tunic and fetched a pot of food from the cooking fire outside.

Bent Feather ate with the concentration of a hungry man. He stuffed the mess of beans, meat, fat and corn into his mouth, wiping his fingers on his forearms to clean them. The meal finished, he took a quiver from a peg and began to check his arrows. They were the wicked barbed arrows used when on the warpath, the shafts painted and feathered according to the individual. The squaw watched.

'There will be war, my husband?'

'There will be war.' He tested the fastening of an arrow head. 'Ten days ago I left to watch the white men, yesterday they began to build the shining rails again. The peace has been broken.'

'Red Arrow is a Great Chief,' she said, her voice devoid of emotion. 'He may yet find a way to avoid the death of our warriors.'

'A warrior is never afraid to die.' Bent Feather looked up in sudden understanding. 'You think of our son, Grave Eagle.'

'He is never from my thoughts.'

'He is a brave boy and will pass his initiation and be a fine warrior. He will ride the warpath and gather many coup. He will take a squaw and she will give him many sons.'

'Or he will feed the vultures.'

'Speak not of that.' Bent Feather lifted his hand as if to strike the woman, then lowered it. 'To talk of death is bad and offends the spirits. Many charms have I given Grave Eagle and he will fight as a man should. He shall not know fear and that is as it should be, for what man need fear so well-trodden a path and many have departed for the Happy Hunting Grounds before him.' He chuckled. 'Smile, wife, you will yet be proud of your son.'

'I am proud of all my children,' she

said quietly. 'To me, as to all, they are the future of our people. To see them die and to wail at their passing is a knife in my heart.'

'You speak true words,' said the warrior gravely. 'And yet some things must be. The land is ours and was our fathers' before us.' He tested the last arrow, replaced it in the quiver then rose to his feet. 'I go to the Council,' he said importantly. 'May the spirits guide our tongues.'

'Good fortune attend you,' said the squaw. She watched him go, warm in the knowledge of his affection, and smiled as she reached for the tunic. Bent Feather was a good man and provided well. Never had they known much hunger and there was always blankets against the winter chill. Two sons she had given him and that was well for sons could ride with their fathers while daughters had to remain in the village and prepare the skins, cook the food and attend to the children.

And yet, daughters did not die from the white man's bullets, the arrows of other tribes, the rifles the white traders gave in exchange for furs and the yellow iron they prized so highly.

She sighed and her fingers, worn with much toil, sewed beads to the tunic meant for her eldest son.

The Council consisted of elders and those deemed worthy to speak. Such men were warriors who had gathered many coup and so earned the respect of their people. An old man, merely because he was old, was not in esteem. A man had to prove himself, prove that his courage and valour were high, that he was a man in the true Indian sense of the word before he could sit in Council.

Even then the Council could give no orders, command no obedience. No Indian could ever force another Indian to do what he did not wish to do. Chiefs held their power only as long as they proved themselves cunning and skilful in war, able to provide the village with plenty of meat and blankets, flour and loot from the continual little wars between tribes, against the white men, or even against the distant Mexicans. War, to the Indians, was a game, a way of life. War was essential if the young men were to prove their valour, for without war, there would be no chance of collecting coup.

Bent Feather ducked inside the big, Council tepee, took his place in the circle around the small, central fire and, legs crossed, waited with Indian patience.

Around him the elders and foremost warriors assembled, all dressed in their full regalia, all feathered with the marks of their proven courage.

A feather was granted for the taking of a scalp, for riding foremost into battle, for being the first to touch an enemy with a bare hand. Other feathers were granted for various acts of bravery, the killing of a foe bare-handed, the stealing into an enemy camp and returning undetected and with a scalp.

One of the highest awards was the sash which Red Arrow wore. The wearer of a sash not only earned it but had to continue to earn it. He would ride into battle, dismount, thrust his lance through the long, trailing end of the sash and then fight off all who came against him. He himself was not permitted to remove the lance and so free himself, only a friend could do that. The wearing of a sash showed that the man was high in proved courage and worthy to be a chief.

The Shaman, the medicine man of the tribe, the healer and witch-doctor, the Indian equivalent to a religious advisor, came into the centre of the circle. He wore a heavy fur coat and a grotesque mask carved from wood and painted to resemble a dog. He carried a hollow gourd filled with a few dried peas and, as he danced around the circle, he rattled the gourd. The capering and rattling were to drive away the evil spirits which could twist the hearts and minds of men so that they spoke with forked tongues. He finished his ceremony, stepped back and handed Red Arrow a stone pipe.

Red Arrow lit the pipe at the fire, blew a puff of smoke to the east, the west, the north and south, puffed smoke towards the sky and towards the ground. He passed it to the man on his right and, slowly, the pipe of peace passed round the circle. The circle completed, Red Arrow commenced speaking.

He spoke gravely and to the point. He passed over the history of the dealings the Sioux had had with the white men. He spoke of the early settlers, their wars, their promises and the broken agreements. He spoke of many things but all bearing on the same subject. Listening to him, Bent Feather and the others knew that he had given much thought to the words and that they came from his heart.

'A warrior who tried to hold too many horses must not wail if some are stolen,' said Red Arrow. 'To the Indian the stealing of a horse is a fine thing, a good thing, it is part of our way of life. Many a warrior has played the game of stealing horses both from Indians and white men. Is this not so?'

'It is so,' Brown Rock, an Indian with many coup as his feathers signified, grunted in agreement.

'If such a warrior stealing horses is caught then he is taken and put to death and his scalp ornaments the tepee of the man who found him.' Red Arrow glanced round the circle of grave-faced men. 'When the white men find an Indian stealing their horses they shoot him. If the white men find a white man stealing their horses they hang him. This I have seen and I speak with a straight tongue.'

'I also.' Bent Feather shifted restlessly as he admitted the truth of the chief's words. What was Red Arrow driving at?

'To us the stealing of horses is a game. If a warrior wins the game then he is praised and no one will think badly of him or try to hurt him. To steal a horse is a great deed and played by many. But to the white man the stealing of horses is a crime. They do not steal horses as the Indians do. Their young men are not taught how to crawl into a corral and select the best mount, to seize it without sound, and to ride it away undetected. Their young men are not taught these things as the Indians are.'

'Red Arrow speaks the truth.' said Brown Rock. 'But to me he is as a stream which wanders far before arriving at the sea. It would be better for Red Arrow to speak as a thrown lance.'

'I will so speak,' said the old chief. He sighed as he looked at the Council. White men would have grasped his point. Would these?

'I have spoken of horses,' he said. 'Now let me speak of land. As the stealing of horses is to an Indian, so is the stealing of land to a white man. They steal and no one blames them. They take what is not theirs to take and they are praised in the lodges of their people. They take from each other when they are able and are thought of highly because of it. They take from the Indian and all white men say they do right and good.'

'If a man comes into my tepee,' said Brown Rock slowly. 'And from my tepee takes my bow, my arrows, my rifle or anything that is mine, he dies.'

Brown Rock stared around the Council. 'He dies by torment and the knives of the women and all will see that he so dies. Even our enemies the Comanche, the Cheyenne, the Apache, will take such a man should he fly to them and return him for death. Is this true speaking?'

'It is true,' said Bent Feather. 'If a man steals a horse belonging to his own tribe then that man dies in the same way. To steal from others is good. To steal from each other is bad and must not be.' He made an impatient gesture. 'These things are known even to the children. Why talk we of them now?'

'If a man is touched by Manitou,' said Red Arrow quietly, 'do we torment him? We leave him alone to live in peace.' He was speaking of insanity, a thing so rare among the Indians that any unfortunate suffering from mental affliction was deemed to have been touched by the Great God Manitou and be almost sacred.

'Has Manitou touched the white men?' Brown Rock snorted. 'You speak words of love for the Long Knives, Red Arrow. It comes to me that this Council has forgotten why it was assembled.'

'The shining rails are coming into our land,' said Bent Feather. 'This thing I have seen with my own eyes. Yet Red Arrow told us that the paper he received from the Chief of the Long Knives promised that this land would be ours for all time.' He looked around the Council. 'Red Arrow speaks with a straight tongue,' he said deliberately. 'He told us true words. But those words are no longer true. The white man has broken his promise as he has broken the promises he made in other days. The white man speaks with a false tongue. The white man must die.'

'They must die!' repeated Brown Rock and the cry was repeated by others.

'Peace!' Red Arrow lifted his hand. 'Words do not kill and saying a thing does not make that thing so. Are we women that we talk and think the thing is good as done? The white man must die, says Bent Feather, and you also Brown Rock, and you, and you. The white man must die.' The Chief snorted with contempt. 'As well to say the mountains must level themselves or the buffalo come into the village to be eaten. Who will do this thing?'

'The Sioux have many warriors,' said Bent Feather. 'There will be more. We have many horses, many guns, many arrows. We can kill the white men who are building the shining rails and will kill them until they are all gone and no more come.'

'This has been tried,' said Red Arrow,

'against my wishes and against the peace we made with the white man, some warriors rode against the men with the instruments of glass and iron who came to measure the land. Those men died, and the warriors, where are they now? Dead, all dead, and many women wailed in the tepees at their passing.'

'That was many moons ago,' said Brown Rock uncomfortably. His own brother had ridden out against the surveyors and had not returned. 'A score of moons has passed since that time. It is best forgotten.'

'Nothing can be forgotten,' said Red Arrow sternly. 'We were at peace with the Long Knives and they killed the men who measured the land. They rode against he who escaped and then they died, all died. They died and then more men came to measure the land and the shining rails followed them.' He paused. 'The Chief of the Long Knives, General Clarke, he came with many men and spoke along with me and the Council.

For the death of the men he forgave me. He did not burn our villages or shoot our warriors. He respected the treaty and said that we had not broken it.'

'He spoke with an oiled tongue,' snapped Brown Rock. 'He said that the men who measured the land did no more than that. The game they killed was the game they ate and that was good for none can deny another if hunger bites at the belly. So we allowed others to measure the land and did not harm them. They gave us gifts, much tobacco, rifles, ammunition, blankets and beads. They came and they went but, after they had gone, the shining rails moved towards us. They are still moving towards us.'

'Where the shining rails go men follow,' said Bent Feather. 'They will come like the sand of the sea and they will bring their squaws and their children, their horses and the horned cattle. They will build towns where the buffalo roam and they will take this land as their own. This I see and promise.'

Other warriors gave deep grunts signifying approval. Red Arrow sat for a long time in silence, his mind working on the problem. To call the tribes to war would be easy. The drums would beat over the prairie, fires would be lit in the villages, warpaint mixed and worn and all the warriors would ride like screaming devils down on to the scattered settlements and railroad camps. Blood would flow and houses would burn.

And then?

Red Arrow knew what would happen then. He knew the one great weakness of his people, their total inability to accept discipline. They would ride the warpath only as long as it suited them. They would ride and kill and then break away satisfied with what they had done. War, to the Indians, was a series of coups, little conflicts in which a few men died and some were wounded. The war-parties met, fought, and then rode away again, the war over and the conflict ended.

But the white men didn't fight like that.

The white man fought and fought and never stopped — until their enemies were defeated. They fought because they had to fight. A white soldier couldn't just go home when he felt like it, refuse to obey an order because he had other things to do. A white soldier was part of a whole, a unit, a cog in a machine. An Indian was an individual first, last and all the time. The greatest trouble any Indian Chief had was in welding the tribes together and getting them to act under his orders. Only a Chief of exceptional courage as proved by his coup could do that.

Red Arrow was such a Chief.

He listened to the conversation springing up around the circle then turned to the Sharman. The medicine man stepped forward, rattling the gourd and silence fell as the warriors waited for the Chief to speak.

'Hear my words,' he said. 'Listen, weigh them well. If we fight we die, our warriors' blood will spill and the squaws will mourn their lost ones. Winter will come and with it cold and hunger. Without warriors to hunt the buffalo and find game many will die from the hunger of their bellies. Is this true?'

They nodded, it was true.

'The white men have many cattle, much flour, many blankets and houses of wood and stone. They do not fear the winter. They will fight and live in the winter as the summer. They will follow us into the hills where there is no game. They will chase us over the prairie. They will catch us and we will die. Is this true?'

Again they nodded.

'Then to war with the white man is bad. Always to war with them is bad for, whenever the Indian has fought the white man, the Indian has died.'

'The white men die also,' said Brown

Rock. 'See the scalps hanging in my tepee if you doubt that.'

'For every white man who dies many Indians die,' said Red Arrow quietly: 'Beyond the mountains to the west and the east are many white men. There are so many white men that if each Indian warrior were to take the scalps of ten times ten hand-counts of them still there would be more. If one Indian died for every ten times ten hand-counts of the white men then we would all die and still there would be as many white men as we had slain.'

'Are they then as the sand of the sea?' asked Brown Rock.

'They are as the buffalo,' said Red Arrow gravely. 'They are as the ants of the hills, the grass of the prairie. To them there is no end.'

'Red Arrow speaks as a woman,' said Bent Feather. 'He is afraid of shadows. Where are these many white men? Here? They are not here. They cannot harm us. We will rid the plains of them and the rest will be afraid to come against us. I have spoken.'

'Am I a woman?' Red Arrow rose to his full height. 'Is this the sash of a woman? Are these feathers the coup of a woman?' He stared round the Council. 'Bent Feather talks as a child.'

'He talks as a child,' agreed Brown Rock. 'but even a child can show the way of manhood. We must fight or be crushed.'

'Say you all so?'

They nodded, grunting to signify agreement. To them it was simple and they could not understand deep policy. Thieves were killed. The white men were stealing the very land they had given. The white men must be killed.

'Hear my words.' Red Arrow paused, staring into the fire. 'War is a thing which time will not change. We can fight today or wait and fight tomorrow. Today we are few with little food and few rifles. Tomorrow we could be many with much dried meat, many blankets, many guns. I shall send messengers to our brothers of the plains. I will send word to our enemies the Comanche, the Cheyenne, the Apache and call them to a Great Council. We will talk with them and smoke the pipe of peace. We will talk and bury the hatchet. We will store food and collect our strength and then, when all else has failed, we will sound the war-drums and ride against the Long Knives. We will rise as one and strike as one and, if we must, we will die as one. Are my words good?'

'They are the words of a fox, an eagle, the words of a Great Chief.' Brown Rock looked at the others, his eyes shining. 'Truly Red Arrow is a man gifted in cunning and fit to be Chief of all the Sioux. I walk with Red Arrow!'

'And I!' said Bent Feather and the others echoed his words. Red Arrow held up his hand.

'Hold!' He stared at them for a long moment. 'This is what we will do for a wise warrior carries a spare bowstring. We will do as I have said and ready ourselves against the time of battle. But, at the same time, I will ask for pow-wow with the Long Knife General Clarke. I will tell him of the broken treaty and ask him to halt the movement of the shining rails.'

'War!' yelled Brown Rock. 'I speak for war!'

'Listen to Red Arrow.' said Bent Feather. 'Listen to the words of our Great Chief.'

'To die is a thing any man can do at any time,' said Red Arrow. 'Let us act like the snake in this thing. Let us talk with the Long Knives and see if they can do with words and papers what we cannot do except with war. Let us wait and see if the white men speak wholly with a false tongue. It may be that our words will prevail and, if so, then many lives will be spared and our squaws will not have cause for wailing.'

'Words!' Brown Rock was disappointed. 'Are we women to waste time in idle talk?'

'On a long journey two horses are better than one,' said Red Arrow. 'A hunter does not shoot his last arrow until he has thrown a stone. We will walk with cunning in this matter. We will obey the treaty and see what the white men will do. If they keep their word then we will live in peace. But if they prove false then we will rise and kill.'

He stared at the Council, wanting them to agree and yet knowing that they were like impatient children who could only see a little way into the future.

'It will take time for us to hold a Great Council,' he pointed out. 'It will take many moons for food to be dried and stored, the warriors to obtain guns, the squaws to tan and treat hides against the time of bitter cold. Live against the day of the battle but, while we work to that end, I will treat with the General of the Long Knives.'

'I will walk with Red Arrow,' said Bent Feather. 'My son, Grave Eagle, will be a man within two moons, I would have him ride with me.'

'I walk with Red Arrow,' said Brown

Rock. 'His words are strong medicine.'

One by one the members of the Council arose, gave allegiance and left the big tepee. All went well until only the Shaman and Red Arrow were left.

'You spoke well,' said the Shaman. He removed his mask and showed features almost identical with those of the Chief. Lame Horse was brother to Red Arrow but, because of an accident when young, walked stiffly and could not ride the warpath.

'I spoke as my heart told me,' said the Chief. He stared thoughtfully into the fire. 'You are wise,' he said at last. 'Men say that you can read the future in the movements of the stars. Have you read what will happen to our people?'

'I read the future only as any man can tell what is to come,' said the Shaman. 'Corn is planted and all know that corn will grow. Clouds hide the smiling face of the sun and the cold winds blow from the north, it is a simple thing to say that winter is on its way. Darkness rises from the east and the sun falls into the sea to die and be born again. Does it take a Shaman to say that it is night?'

'Is the future of the Sioux as simple a thing?'

'If grass is trampled and no grass sown, will the grass not die and be as it never was? If the buffalo are slain and no buffalo born, where will be the great herds we know? If Manitou puts out the stars and does not relight them, will there be lights in the sky to guide our feet?'

'You speak true,' said Red Arrow slowly. 'Few children are born to the Sioux for custom keeps a man from his squaw until the first born has seen a score of moons wax and wane. Warriors die and our people grow less each winter. Wars with the white men have made us few so that we can summon few warriors. We are as a dying tree.'

'We are a dying tree,' agreed the Shaman. 'But sometimes a tree can live again — if it is not cut down.' He looked at the Chief. 'Is it better for a bird to live in a cage than not to live at all?'

'Can the eagle live in a cage?' Red Arrow shrugged. 'Time will tell,' he said philosophically. 'All may yet be well.'

He sighed as he stared into the fire.

5

General Robert Clarke was a man who had grown grey in the service of his country. His thin hair swept back from a high forehead and his eyes, a light brown, stared from either side of a face lined and seamed with countless wrinkles. He had fought all through the civil war, seeing his side sweep to victory and then, rather than accept demobilization, had chosen to come west to the borders of the Indian territory.

His garrison consisted of a troop of cavalry and with these few men he was supposed to bring law and order to an impossible area. He did his best but knew, all the time, that his best was not good enough. And, now that the Indians seemed peaceful, the railroad had come to add to his worries.

He looked up from his desk as

an orderly opened the door of his office.

'Yes?'

'Major Lamont to see you, sir,' said the orderly. 'Shall I show him in?'

'Yes. Wait.' The General hesitated. 'Have any men ridden in from Indian country?'

'No, sir.' The orderly looked surprised. 'Are you expecting any?'

'Yes. A couple of men are due in any day now. When they arrive notify me immediately.'

'Yes, sir.' The orderly, a weather-beaten sergeant who had served with the general long enough to adopt certain liberties, twisted his head to stare behind him. 'And Major Lamont?'

'Show him in.'

Major Lamont was a civilian who, after he had left the army, had taken a job with the railroad. He was a big, beefy, red-faced man with a driving personality and a consuming impatience to get things done. He strode into the office, threw his hat into one chair, sat in another and glared at the general.

'When are you people going to get rid of the Indians?'

'When?' Clarke lifted the lid of a box, took out a cigar, rolled it between his fingers, lit it and settled back with a sigh of contentment. His appearance was deceptive. He didn't like the railroad man and he knew that the feeling was returned. 'Why should we get rid of them?'

'You know why.' Lamont scowled at the other's lack of hospitality and lit one of his own cigars. 'They're slowing down construction, that's why.'

'Are they?' Clarke raised his eyebrows. 'Would you mind telling me just how they are doing that?'

'By being alive,' said Lamont bluntly. He leaned forward. 'Look, Clarke, this is how it is. I've got a mixed crew of men out there who are trying to lay steel. I've got Irish, Germans, Mexicans, the whole damn world in miniature. All right. So they start work and look up and see an Indian watching them. That's all, just sitting on a horse well out of rifle shot watching them. So they try and forget it but, every time they look up, there he is. They talk and some old-timer begins to frighten them with tales of the old days, you know, burying a man in sand and smearing his head with molasses so that the ants eat his skull clean or tying a man with rawhide and propping open his eyes with twigs so that he has to stare into the sun until he's blind. Tales like that.'

'So?'

'So it gets on their nerves. They can't concentrate on what they're doing so they slow down and work suffers.'

'You did say that you had a crew of men, didn't you?' The general's sarcasm was obvious.

'Sure they're men, that's why they worry. They know we're driving the railroad through Indian territory and they know that the Indians aren't going to like it. They can't work and think about what may happen to them if the

93

Indians attack at the same time. It's getting so that half of them don't sleep at night.'

'Too bad.' The general shook his head, he was enjoying this. 'What do you want me to do, rock them to sleep?'

'I want you to get rid of those Indians,' snapped Lamont. 'At least get rid of the ones watching us.'

'I can't do that.'

'Why not?'

'This is Indian territory, they have as much right there as you have. In fact they have all the right to be here and you have no right at all.' Clarke shrugged. 'I can't see what you expect me to do. Surely you've tried to settle the problem.'

'I have.' Lamont was grim. 'I offered a bonus to any man who could bring that redskin down. A dozen men fired fifty rounds and couldn't touch him. Then a bunch of the men got together, found some horses and took after him.'

'They didn't catch him, naturally,'

said the general. 'What happened?'

'We had to send out to rescue the men who'd ridden off.' Lamont bit at his cigar. 'They got themselves lost. I lost two days' work over that and, when it was over, danged if that Indian wasn't back on the skyline watching us.'

'Probably he was having fun,' said the general. He became thoughtful. 'Look, Lamont, let's get this thing straight. That Indian was doing no harm. I'd say that he was just curious. Had no attacks of scalpings, have you?'

'Not yet.'

'I take it that the men are armed?'

'I've issued a six-gun to each man and posted guards with rifles,' admitted Lamont. 'Hell, General, I know that the men are safe enough, you needn't tell me that, but what difference does it make? They won't feel secure until they see some uniforms. I want you to let me have some soldiers to ride around the camp and stop the men worrying about losing their hair. The way things are going winter will be here before we know it and I'm behind schedule as it is.'

Clarke shook his head.

'You won't do it?'

'No.'

'Hell!' Lamont crushed his cigar in one big hand. 'What's the army for, that's what I'd like to know?'

'The army is here to protect the lives and property of settlers and other white men,' said Clarke. 'If I waste men riding at your railhead then someone's going to go unprotected. The way things are you've a lot of armed men and should be able to take care of any Indian attack. Not everyone is so lucky. I've got to patrol a big area with a few men and I just can't afford to let you have any. Sorry.'

'Is that your last word, General?'

'Yes.'

'All right.' Lamont heaved himself to his feet and grabbed his hat. 'Don't be surprised if you get a message from back east ordering you to change your mind. A lot of people think that getting the railroad through is of prime importance. Once we finish, then this part of the country can be developed. Those people aren't going to let a few lousy Indians stand in the way of progress.'

'Those people aren't trying to farm a few acres or start a new life out here,' said Clarke grimly. 'If they were maybe they'd think differently about robbing the little men of their protection.'

'I can't worry about that,' said Lamont. 'My job is to lay steel.'

'And mine is to keep the peace.' Clarke stared at Lamont. 'Be reasonable, man. You've at least a hundred armed men working for you. Surely a handful of soldiers can't make all that difference?'

'No,' admitted Lamont. He shrugged. 'As an old army man I understand your problem, but that doesn't alter things. I'm losing men too fast to be choosy about what I do to get the job done. Most of the workers have never been out of a town before. Some of them are jailbirds, deserters, half-breeds and morons. Most of them are superstitious. I know and you know that a hundred armed men can beat back any surprise attack but these men aren't soldiers. All they can think of is the Indians riding down and lifting their hair.' He hesitated. 'Look, General, I don't want to ride you too hard about this. How about you letting me have a few men just for show?'

'Perhaps.' Clarke was willing to make a compromise. He knew too well the power back east behind the railroad. 'When will you have completed your link and connected up with the main branch?'

'Before winter,' said Lamont. 'The men back east are working without trouble to push the railroad forward. We here have started a new camp and we'll lay steel westwards. There are other camps scattered along the route and sleepers and rails have been freighted to them. Naturally, as the line extends the trains can come further and further. As soon as the connection is made back east the trains can come all the way to Fort Hemridge.' He chuckled. 'That'll be the day when this part of the country is finally civilized. First the railroad, then the settlers, then the trade with merchants and the rest.'

Clarke nodded and, rising, crossed to a map which hung against one wall. With his forefinger he traced the thin, red line of the proposed railway.

'You'll have no trouble eastwards,' he said. 'Not until you pass Fort Hemridge. What will happen when you push on into Red Arrow's country I wouldn't like to guess.' He turned as the orderly opened the door. 'Yes?'

'Two men have just reported in, sir,' said the sergeant. He looked at Lamont. 'If you're free, sir?'

'A moment.' Clarke held out his hand to the railroad boss. 'Try to calm your men, Lamont. I don't want any trigger-happy fools starting something they can't finish.'

'What we start we'll finish,' promised

Lamont grimly. 'You'll send some men?'

'Yes.'

'When?'

'Soon.'

'How about sending them now?' Lamont grinned. 'Let's have no trouble over this, General. I'm not asking for much, just a handful of soldier-boys to ride around and look busy. If they can keep that dawn Indian out of sight I'll be more than satisfied.'

'All right.' Clarke opened the door. 'Orderly!'

'Sir!'

'Send Sergeant Watson in to see me.' Clarke looked at Lamont. 'You can leave it with me.'

'I'm in no hurry,' said Lamont. He grinned and lit a fresh cigar. 'An old army saying, General, which you will probably appreciate. If you want a thing done then do it yourself, maybe we should add to that. If you want a thing done wait until someone's done it.'

Clarke ignored him. As an old soldier

and an officer he had had to compromise with politics before. Lamont had the power behind him, men who, if they wished, could break the General and have him transferred to a small forgotten outpost where he could die and never be missed. Without being ambitious Clarke was realistic enough to know that being stubborn was the quickest way to get hurt. He also knew that, to do the most good, he had to be in a position of authority.

He looked up as Sergeant Watson entered the room, saluted and stood at attention. Clarke returned the salute.

'Take twenty men, Sergeant,' he ordered. 'Rations for ten days. Fifty rounds a man. You will ride to the rail-camp and patrol the area. You will not open fire on any Indian for any cause. You will not deviate from your instructions. You will ride patrol, at all times leaving some men visible from the camp, and you will not engage in combat with the Indians unless it is to defend the camp. Is that clear?'

'Yes, sir.'

'Repeat your instructions.'

'We are to ride patrol at the rail-camp,' said the sergeant quickly. 'We are to remain visible to the camp, not to shoot Indians, take no offensive action unless to defend the camp. Correct, sir?'

'Correct.' Clarke nodded to Lamont. 'Satisfied?'

'Sure.' The big man rolled his cigar between his teeth. 'But why worry about rations? The men can mess with the workers and share their grub. And what about if they get attacked?'

'You will not return fire from Indians,' said the General to Watson. 'You will retreat back to the camp if attacked. I don't for one moment expect that you will be but, if you are, those are your orders.'

'Yes, sir. And the rations?'

'Take them. You are not to eat with the workers or sleep in the camp. You understand me, Sergeant?'

'Yes, sir.'

The sergeant saluted, turned on his heel and left the office. Clarke watched him go then stared at Lamont.

'Anything else?'

'Not for now.'

'Then good-day to you. Orderly!'

'Yes, sir?'

'Major Lamont is leaving. You may inform the two men that I will see them now.'

'Yes, sir.' The old sergeant waited until Lamont had left the office before following. He beckoned to the waiting men and, as they passed Lamont, he stared at the taller of the two.

'Wilson?'

'You know me?' Mike Wilson looked at the railroad boss.

'I think so. I've heard of you anyway.' Lamont looked at Sam. 'A friend of yours?'

'That's right.'

'You going in to see the general?'

'Maybe.' Mike stared coldly at the big man. 'What's on your mind?'

'Nothing serious. I'd like to talk to

you after you've finished in there. How about meeting me in the Golden Chance?'

'Why not?' Mike nodded. 'We'll be seeing you.' He nudged Sam once and together they entered the General's office.

Sam had filled out since that night two years ago when he had watched his grandfather die. He had grown in other ways too. Now he walked like a man who knew where he was going. He, like Mike, wore buckskins, fringed and tanned to a surprising softness. Both men were armed with a pair of the long-barrelled frontier Colt .45s and each carried a bowie. Clarke waited until they were seated, offered cigars which Mike accepted and Sam refused, then got down to business.

'What's the position?'

'Fair.' Mike rose and crossed to the map. 'We located a site for the fort just at the edge of this river. It isn't deep and it's not wide but it'll stop attack from that quarter. The slopes are well-wooded so you'll have plenty of building material. The ground is well-supplied with game and on the main route west.' He dropped his hand. 'There are probably better places for a fort but not many. When are you due to move?'

'I don't know.' Clarke scowled at the map. 'I'm stuck here until replacements arrive and I'm not sure when that will be.'

'They authorized you building a new fort, didn't they?'

'They did,' admitted Clarke. 'But the Indians have been so quiet lately that they probably think it won't be necessary.'

'They're wrong,' said Mike flatly. 'We've ridden deep into Indian territory and the place is full of unrest. You know what I mean, warriors trailing us all the time, not doing anything but just watching. Had they been on the warpath we wouldn't have stood a chance. If the railroad tries to push on without that new fort then the workers will be wiped out to the last man.'

'I know it,' admitted Clarke. He ground one fist in the palm of his hand. 'It's this delay which is worrying me. The railroad is pushing on without waiting for the fort to be built. If they push too fast and too far, or if replacements don't arrive, or the fort isn't built, then we'll be helpless against a sudden attack. It's a wonder that Red Arrow hasn't broken loose already. He knows as well as I do that the railroad is breaking the treaty and yet nothing has happened. I don't like it.'

Mike shrugged, drawing at his cigar, saying nothing. Sam, his eyes alert, looked at the tall man, seemed about to say something, then changed his mind. Clarke caught the gesture and looked at the young man.

'Well, Sam?'

'Nothing.'

'No?' The General smiled. He remembered the day when both men had ridden into Fort Hemridge, Mike with his laconic account of the massacre of the surveying party and subsequent wiping out of the attacking Indians, Sam filled with the desire for revenge against each and every Indian. Mike had tamed that madness, had taught the young man that life was too big for small things to be allowed to rule a man's life. He had taken the youngster under his protection and, together, they had ridden as official scouts and hunters for the garrison.

'I was just thinking,' said Sam. 'Couldn't you stop the railroad until the fort is built?'

'Trying to stop the railroad would only get me put on half-pay,' said the General. 'That's no solution.' He frowned. 'Well, I guess you've done all you can do. You've scouted the Territory, found a good site for the new fort if and when it's ever built, and returned alive. No man could have done more.' He ruffled the papers on his desk. 'Just at the moment there isn't much for you to do around here but . . .'

'Never mind that, General.' Mike puffed smoke and stared at the coiling plumes. 'We're finished with working for the army. Sam and me have a hankering to go buffalo hunting, seems there's big money to be made from hides and meat.'

'That's right.' A shadow crossed the general's face. 'Where were you thinking of operating?'

'With the other hunters.' Mike rose to his feet. 'Don't worry about us, General. We'll be all right.'

'I'll make out your pay.' Clarke picked up a pen and wrote on a form. 'Give this to the paymaster and he'll settle what we owe you. Need anything else?'

'Nothing I can't buy.'

'Did I ask you to pay for it?' Clarke frowned. 'How about ammunition, blankets, stuff like that?'

'Aren't you forgetting something?' Mike stared at the General. 'We aren't working for the army now. If you give us stores without just cause you'll be heading for trouble.' His smile took the sting from the rebuke. 'Thanks, anyway, General, but we've got all we need. Be seeing you.'

He led the way from the office.

6

The Golden Chance, like most frontier saloons, consisted of a long room flanked by the bar and faced by the swing doors. To one end were the gambling tables, the faro bank, poker and monte dealers, a spinning wheel together with the inevitable dice. At the other was a piano, freighted at high cost from St Louis and the piano player, a thin, hollow-chested man who had come west for the sake of his health.

Several small tables together with chairs covered most of the floor but left the space in front of the long bar free for customers who liked to drink, while standing. Major Lamont was leaning against the bar when Mike and Sam entered and he nodded to them, slapping the bar to call the bartender.

'A bottle of the best, Joe, and clean glasses.' He paid for the whiskey and tilted the bottle and poured two glasses full of the potent spirit. He was about to fill the third when Sam stopped him.

'Not for me.'

'You don't drink?'

'No.'

'Odd.' Lamont looked at the youngster. 'Not many men in this part of the world who don't take their liquor.'

'I don't drink,' repeated Sam. He looked at Joe. 'Got any sarsasparilla?'

'Sure.' The bartender ducked under the counter and produced the soft drink.

A bar lounger, leaning on the counter a little way from where Lamont was standing, heard the order and stared as Sam sipped his drink. He grinned and stepped forward. He was just drunk enough to be in the mood for a little fun and Sam seemed to provide a sure butt.

'Why don't someone tell this kid that this place is for men?' He hooked the thumb of his left hand in the cartridge belt around his waist. 'Maybe his Ma doesn't know he's out?'

Sam ignored him.

'Say, you the tall guy!' The lounger looked at Mike. 'You with this kid?'

'Talking to me?' Mike stared at the lounger, his blue eyes cold.

'Sure, I ain't talking to myself.' The man lurched closer. 'What's the idea of bringing this kid in here?'

'Cut it out, Butch,' said the bartender. 'A man's got the right to drink what he wants when he wants.'

'Shut your mouth, you!' Something hard and cruel came into Butch's voice. His eyes glittered with sadistic pleasure and Mike guessed that he was a man with a swollen idea of his own importance. He looked at the guns hanging low against the man's thighs, the tied down, open holsters, the smooth butts and the easy way the man's hand rested inches away from the walnut grips of his Colts. The man was a gunslinger, fast on the draw and both willing and eager to shoot.

And he was looking for trouble.

Mike hesitated, looking at Sam then at the gunslinger. He knew the type, knew too that the more Sam yielded the harder he would be pushed. But he knew too that he could not interfere, not until interference was essential.

'I don't like kids who come in here still wet behind the ears,' said Butch coldly. He reached for the bottle, filled the empty glass with whiskey, pushed it towards Sam. 'Have a drink.'

'I don't touch it,' said Sam.

'I've invited you to have a drink,' said Butch sharply. 'I guess that I ain't the sort of man to be ignored. Drink it!'

Sam looked at Butch, then at Mike. He knew that he could take the drink, swallow it, and probably the unpleasantness would be over. Butch would have won his point and be satisfied. Or perhaps he would insist on Sam taking a second drink, a third, more until he was helplessly intoxicated. That would amuse the gunslinger.

'I don't drink,' said Sam quietly. 'I'll thank you to leave me alone.'

'You'll take that drink!' snapped Butch and now his eyes held a feral glitter. 'You'll take it or take what I give you.' His hand dropped to his gun. 'Maybe you'd prefer to dance.'

Sam swallowed, knowing what the man was getting at. He would think it funny to draw his guns and send lead towards the youngster's feet. Sam would have to jump in the air to avoid the bullets, he wouldn't be able to help himself, and if Butch was careless or deliberately cruel, then lead could rip into the soft bones and leave Sam a cripple.

He picked up the glass.

'That's better.' Butch grinned and relaxed as he saw the action. 'Swallow it down.' He stared as Sam lifted the glass.

Sam threw the whiskey directly into his eyes.

Butch screamed as the raw spirit burned his eyes and, blinded, staggered back, his hand clawing at his gun. Sam stepped forward his fist driving against the other's nose. He hit again, his left hand driving deep into the stomach and Butch, stunned and retching, fell back across one of the small tables.

'I don't drink,' said Sam, staring down at the moaning man. 'Remember that.' He turned and went back to the bar.

Butch, clawing at his burning eyes, lay where he had fallen. He was mad with rage and in a killing mood but first he had to clear his sight. Slowly he rose to his feet, his lips writhing as he saw that Sam was facing away from him. He stood, wide legged, his hands hovering over the butts of his guns.

'Greenhorn,' he rasped. 'Go for your irons!' His hands darted downwards, lifted the Colts from their holsters and the long barrels swung towards the youngster.

Flame and lead blasted in the confines of the saloon sending echoes from the raftered roof and causing the gamblers to stiffen where they sat, their hands reaching for their weapons.

Butch, a stunned expression on his face, stood swaying, his unfired guns in his hands. Then he fell, slumping down like a sack of meal, his head thudding against the floor and a small, red-rimmed hole between his eyes.

'Never turn your back on an enemy,' said Mike. Slowly he ejected the spent shell from his Colt and refilled the chamber with a fresh load from his belt.

'You got him,' said Joe the bartender. 'Smack between the eyes.' He stared at Mike. 'You was facing the bar when he climbed to his feet. I saw him go for his irons and you hadn't moved.'

'I saw him in the mirror.' Mike slipped the gun back into its holster. 'You made a mistake, Sam,' he said evenly. 'If you beat a man up then make sure that he can't bushwhack you afterwards. You should have taken his guns. Better yet, never beat a man up. If you've a quarrel with him then kill him. That way you don't have to worry about him any more.'

'You saved my life,' said Sam. He

knew that he would never have been able to draw and fire as fast as the tall man. 'Thanks.'

'That was some shooting!' Lamont dabbed at his forehead. 'I've never seen anything like it.' He looked at Mike. 'I've heard about you but didn't believe half of what I heard. Now I'm changing my mind.'

'How about the body?' Sam stared at the dead man, then at the bartender. Joe shrugged.

'It was self-defence and I'll tell the sheriff so. You don't have to worry. Butch was getting a bit above himself and was due to be cut down. You've done the town a service. Forget it.'

'Let's go into a corner.' Lamont picked up the bottle of whiskey and led the way towards a table set against the wall. Like most men of that day and place he ignored the sudden violence and death as things of no importance. When men carried guns at their waists and were ready and willing to use them, then shootings and violence were a part of living. Butch would be collected, buried, and forgotten.

It was as simple as that.

'What's this proposition you were telling me about?'

Mike sipped his whiskey, accepted a cigar, lit it and stared at Lamont.

'It's simple, you know who I am?'

'Sure.'

'Then I needn't go into a lot of details.' Lamont stared out of the window towards the fort. 'What was your business with Clarke?'

'Private.'

'I'm not asking from curiosity. I've heard tell that the army are going to build a new fort deep in Indian territory. Right?'

'Could be.'

'You don't have to fence with me, Wilson.' Lamont helped himself to more whiskey. 'You know that the railroad is pushing west into Red Arrow's country and you know that it's the army's job to protect it.' He sipped at his glass. 'There are a lot of people back east who want to get this railroad finished. Those people have a lot of influence with the Indian Bureau and Congress. If a new fort is essential then we'll have a new fort. But is it? Would the expense be worth it? The Indians seem quiet enough, even though we've pushed steel into their land.'

'If you want to build that railroad then you'll have to have a new fort,' said Mike flatly.

'That's just your opinion?'

'Yes.'

'You should know what you're talking about,' admitted Lamont. 'You think there's danger of an uprising?'

'I don't think,' said Mike. 'I know. Sam and me rode right across the Indian territory. The Nations are like a powder barrel, one spark and up she goes. I've beaten a trail to the site of the new fort and I've covered the ground pretty well. If you've got any influence back east you'll get the General his replacements so that he can start work on that fort.'

'And if not?'

'It's your funeral.' Mike shrugged. 'I don't have to tell you how vulnerable the railroad is. A couple of braves could rip up a mile of track in a few hours. Or they could derail a train and have themselves some fun with the crew. Clarke's the only man who can stop them.'

'Yes,' said Lamont. He stared at his glass, his forehead furrowed in thought. He lifted his head as the sound of horses came from the street and grinned as a line of soldiers passed the saloon.

Mike stared but said nothing.

'Those soldiers are going to the railhead camp,' said Lamont. 'We'll show those Indians that we mean business.'

'Sure,' said Mike drily. 'With a few dead Indians to drive home the lesson?'

'Why not? We can do without the Indians.'

'Maybe.' Mike shrugged and got down to business. 'You said that you wanted to see me. Why?'

'I want to employ you,' said Lamont. 'I need a scout,' he glanced at Sam, 'a couple of scouts. Good men who can let me know just where the Indians are, what they're doing, things like that.' He told Mike of the trouble he was having at the camp. 'It's no joke, not to the men or to me. All of us would feel better if we had a couple of men working for us.'

'And maybe fetch in a few dead Indians?' Mike shook his head. 'You'd be a fool to try anything like that. At the moment there is peace between Red Arrow and the white men. Break that peace and he'll ride down and wipe out your camp.'

'My men are armed.'

'All right, then why look for trouble when you don't want it?'

'I don't want trouble,' said Lamont sincerely. 'I want to get the railroad built, but I can't do it this way.' He leaned forward. 'Would you be willing to scout for me?'

'No.'

'Why not?'

'Sam and me are going hunting. There's a lot of money to be made from buffalo and I want some of it.' Mike finished his drink and set down the empty glass. 'Tell you what we will do. We'll supply your camp with meat and game, regular rates.'

'I can use a good hunter,' admitted Lamont. 'I'm pushing a new crew west in a couple of days to start laying track. They'll be deep in the Nations and can use meat. Freighting rail will be hard enough without worrying about food. Like to take on the job?'

'Maybe. How far west?'

'Thirty miles from the present camp. They'll start laying rail to the west and we'll catch them up.' Lamont rose. 'Call in at the railhead and see me. I'll give you full details then.' He held out his hand. 'I'll be looking forward to working with you, Wilson.' He left the saloon.

Mike watched him go, smoking

thoughtfully and rolling his cigar. He smiled and looked at Sam.

'Well?'

'He's playing a real deep game,' said Sam. 'Something's brewing in that mind of his. I wouldn't trust him too far.'

'I wouldn't trust him at all,' said Mike. 'I've met Major Lamont before though he doesn't remember it, no reason why he should.' He helped himself to more whiskey. 'It was during the war. We'd captured a small group of Northerners and Lamont was one of them. He was an officer and we accepted his parole. He ran out on us, killing a couple of men in the process.'

'Was that bad?' Sam didn't understand the delicate relationship between opposed officers in time of war. Mike thinned his lips.

'It was very bad,' he said. 'Both for the men who died and the prisoners we took afterwards. We didn't trust any of them after that.' He shrugged, dismissing the incident. 'Now he's working for the railroad and I'll take a bet that he's paid on results. The more track he gets down the higher his bonus. No harm in that but it could lead to trouble. Lamont's the kind of man who'll push on regardless. The type of man who would start an Indian war for the sake of a few extra dollars in the bank.'

'Let's forget it.' said Sam. 'When are we going to start hunting buffalo?'

'Eager to have a crack at the herds?' Mike smiled. 'We'll stock up with what we need and get moving. You can ride straight on and I'll go and have a talk with Lamont. No sense in throwing away the chance to pick up some money by supplying his camp with meat. If we don't supply them then others will.' He took another drink and rose. 'Let's go to the gunsmith's.'

The gunsmith kept his wares in a small shop close to the fort. He was an old man, skilled in his trade and was busy filing the sear of a Colt when Mike and Sam entered. He put down his file and nodded towards the two men.

'Anything I can do for you?'

'We need some gear for buffalo hunting,' said Sam quickly. He had looked forward to the venture for a long time and was impatient to get started. 'Can you fix us up?'

'Certainly.' The old gunsmith reached under his counter. 'You'll need a heavy rifle, a Sharps is the one usually used.' He placed the heavy weapon on the counter. 'Here's a good one.'

'Wait a minute.' Mike hefted the weapon. 'I've got my own ideas as to buffalo hunting and I'd like to give them a try.' He put down the Sharps rifle. It was a cumbersome affair, unequalled for long-distance shooting and throwing a slug of lead some two inches long. The shock impact was terrific but the rifle was so heavy, almost twenty pounds, that it had to be fired from a stand. One of the great disadvantages of it was that, with the overloaded charge, the gun had to be cooled frequently with wet rags. A hundred rounds fired from a Sharps on continuous use usually meant that the weapon was ruined by heat-distortion.

'All buffalo hunters use a Sharps,' said the gunsmith. 'It's the right gun for the job.'

'I don't think so.' Mike stared around the shop. 'I've seen buffalo and spoken to hunters and I think that there's a better way of killing them.'

'I doubt it.' The gunsmith was stubborn. 'I've sold lots of them rifles and never had a complaint yet. Why, there's a party fitting out right now, three men and a couple of wagons. They figure on using Sharps.'

'That's their business,' said Mike. He became thoughtful. 'Another party, you say?'

'That's right. An old man and his two sons. The Blakes from Missouri I think they said.' The old man craned his head. 'Looks like they're coming this minute.'

Mike turned as the door opened and an elderly man entered the shop. He was withered, bearded, and yet his eyes were youthful and his step young. He stared at Mike, then looked at the gunsmith.

'Got my gear?'

'Sure.' The gunsmith reached behind him. 'All ready.'

'Wait a minute.' Mike touched the oldster on the arm. 'My name's Wilson, this is Sam my partner. I hear that you're going after buffalo.'

'That's right. Me and my two boys Jud and Zeke are leaving right away.' He looked shrewdly at Mike. 'Why?'

'Ever hunted buflalo before?'

'Nope.'

'Have your boys?'

'No, but we can learn.'

'Sure, but it may cost you money to do the learning.' Mike jerked his head. 'Let's go somewhere and talk.'

'My boys are waiting outside with the wagons,' said the old man. He hesitated. 'I guess that we can spare a little time.'

Out in the street he led the way towards a couple of wagons drawn by teams of sturdy mules. Mike looked at the equipment and nodded. He followed the old man into the lead wagon and was introduced to the two young men.

'I'll make this short,' said Mike. 'I hear that you're after buffalo, so are we. I hear that you haven't had any experience in hunting the beasts. I have. I suggest we get together.' He looked at the old man. 'How do you feel about it?'

'Keep talking,' said the old man. Zeke, the oldest of the two boys, looked impatient. 'Come on, Pa,' he said. 'We don't want to waste no more time.'

'Old Abel knows what he's doing,' said the oldster. 'Quit pawing the ground.'

'Listen,' said Mike. 'I've got some money, enough to buy in. With five of us we can do better than with just two or three. How about if we buy one wagon and team from you, chip in for half the gear and then work as a team? Well split the take five ways. Right?'

'Maybe.' Abel stared at the tall man. 'Sounds reasonable anyways. Now tell us why you figure that you can hunt better than we can?'

'How many head do you hope to kill?' asked Mike. 'A hundred? Two hundred? A day, of course, have you any idea?'

'We reckon on a hundred head,' said Abel.

'Youll be lucky to get fifty,' said Mike. 'Maybe you'll get twenty-five, maybe twenty. Can you make the trip pay on that figure?'

'I don't know.' Abel glanced at his sons. 'We've heard tell of bigger bags than that.'

'Sure,' said Mike. 'But remember this, the average hunter goes out with maybe four wagons, drivers, stockmen, cook, and others to skin the kill. He sells the meat and hides for what he can get, splits the take into two parts, then starts paying out. One half the take goes to the helpers, the other half goes to the hunter from which he has to pay for all gear and equipment used. The point is that as all he does is to shoot, he maybe can bring down a hundred head a day. Maybe.'

'We're all pretty good shots,' said Abel. 'With three of us at the guns we should do better than the average hunter.'

'And who skins the kill? Salts the hides and moves the camp?' Mike shrugged. 'You can't have it both ways.'

'That's right,' said Abel. He looked thoughtful. 'What's your idea?'

'We'll all work as a team, all work in camp, do the skinning and any other chores. We can send off one wagon with a load of hides and meat and still operate using the other.' Mike glanced at Sam. 'Here's the idea. You handle the teams and wagons and Sam and I do the killing. We know the Indian Nations and know the habits of the buffalo. I reckon that we can clear twenty-five head a day every day during the season.' He paused. 'There's one other thing. Five men are better against

Indians than two or three.'

'That's right.' Old man Abel puffed out his cheeks. 'You talk sense, and you seem to know what you're doing.' He glanced at Jud and Zeke. 'How about it, boys, do we get together?'

They nodded, both impressed by the tall man and his silent companion, his air of assurance and his obvious knowledge.

'All right.' Abel held out his hand. 'You be camp boss and we'll do as you say. Now we'd better get the gear from the gunsmith's and get on our way.'

'I'll attend to the gear,' said Mike. 'I'll bet that you've bought some Sharps and ammunition for them. Right?'

'That's right.'

'Those guns fire slugs eight to the pound,' said Mike. 'That's a lot of weight to carry and the ammunition is expensive. I've got a better idea, will you trust me?'

'Sure, but we need rifles to kill the buffalo, don't we?'

'No.'

'No?' Abel looked baffled. 'You aim to scare them to death?'

'No.' Mike jumped down from the wagon. 'Sam, you go and get the horses. Abel, you come with me.' He led the way back to the gunsmith's.

Inside he cut short the gunsmith's attempts to sell him weapons the gunsmith thought he should have.

'All we want are weapons to kill buffalo,' he said. 'We've got Winchesters and Colts. Have you got any shotguns?'

'Shotguns?' The gunsmith looked blank. 'What you want them for?'

'Have you got any?'

'Sure, plenty of them, but I thought you said you was going after buffalo?'

'We are.' Mike grinned at Abel. 'I know what I'm doing,' he said.

'I hope so.' Abel shrugged, having decided to trust the tall man, he didn't want to argue. That could come later if need be.

'Show me some shotguns. I want breech-loaders with extra heavy barrels and large bores.' He waited as the gunsmith placed several on the counter. 'Good. Now I want some shells, some powder, caps and equipment to do my own loading. Can you supply that?'

The gunsmith could and he placed the articles on the counter with the guns.

'Anything else?'

'Some slugs for the shells. I want them to be over an ounce to the shell. If you've got a bullet mould and some lead it will do as well, we can cast our own.'

The gunsmith shook his head as he fetched the lead and mould. Abel, his eyes anxious, touched Mike on the arm.

'I ain't questioning what you're doing,' he said. 'But how do you aim to kill a buffalo with a shotgun?'

'Simple. Point it at the animal and pull the trigger.'

'But a shotgun's got no range to speak of.'

'Then we get closer to the target before pulling the trigger,' said Mike calmly.

Abel sighed and shook his head.

7

The initiation was over and Bent Feather was as proud as only a father can be. His eldest son, Grave Eagle, had passed the rigorous tests and was now in his full manhood. Soon he would ride his first warpath and kill his first enemy. Then he would be a true warrior with his foot on the path to greatness. Bent Feather smiled as he stared at his son, his mind, like that of all fathers anywhere, painting the future for his boy.

'It is good,' he said in his deep voice. 'I have a horse which shall be yours, a bow made from the finest horn and arrows feathered from an eagle. Also there is a rifle which I took from a white man. You shall not ride the warpath with empty hands.'

'I thank Bent Feather,' said Grave Eagle for, now that he was a man, he was no longer a child and did not speak as a child. He was a warrior, equal to the man who had given him birth and addressed him as such.

'It will be my pleasure for you to ride at my side,' said Bent Feather. 'Together we shall rise against our enemies and many will be the scalps hanging from the village poles. Say that it is your wish also, Grave Eagle, so that my heart may be glad.'

'It is my wish,' said Grave Eagle. He turned as the Shaman came towards them. Lame Horse was not in his regalia, he had discarded it after the initiation during which he had tested the young men for their fitness for manhood. Some had failed and these would have to wait another year until the time of the next testing. Until that time they would be regarded as children, unable to marry, unable to ride the warpath or wear warpaint. All would pass the next time for they would be helped by the Shaman and their knowledge of what was to come.

Sometimes, though not often, the Shaman gave a numbing drink to those who had big spirits but weak bodies and so helped them more than others. For it was not good that a man should be shamed or his parents cast down.

'Grave Eagle will make a great warrior,' said the Shaman resting his hand on the young warrior's shoulder. 'I see the spirits hover above his head ready to strengthen his arm and to protect him from his enemies. You should be proud of such a son, Bent Feather. The grown tree should not rob the sapling of the sun. It should offer shade if the sun grows too hot but not take the sun away.'

'Grave Eagle is a man and shall ride a man's path,' said Bent Feather. 'I shall not stand in his sun but be ready to call on his shade.'

'You speak with a straight tongue.' Lame Horse was pleased at the way Bent Feather had turned his words. Little to fear from this warrior, he would not try to gain coup at the expense of his son. Rivalry between warriors was good as it made for bravery, but rivalry between old warriors and young was bad because it made the youths take risks beyond their skill.

'What news of the messengers who carried the call to a Great Council?' Bent Feather was anxious to keep abreast with the news.

'They have returned. All will come, the Cheyenne, the Comanche, even the Apache. They will assemble two moons from now. During that time no hand may be lifted against the white man, no hand against our red brothers. We must hunt and store food and fashion weapons against the day of need. These are the words of Red Arrow.'

'Two moons.' Bent Feather rubbed his moccasins in the dirt. 'It is long.'

'It will pass. In the meanwhile you and this new warrior have work that may be to your liking.' The Shaman smiled. 'Red Arrow asks that you ride out to watch the white men. You will send Grave Eagle back to bring word or ride back yourself. Others are doing this for Red Arrow but you are skilled in devious ways and it would be well for Grave Eagle to learn from a master.'

The compliment was just and well deserved. Bent Feather was cunning at laying a false trail, skilled at watching while unwatched, and knew how to assess numbers, report intelligently, and not run foolish risks. He nodded, not smiling, and led the way towards his tepee. His son, because he was now a man, could no longer live with his mother but had his own tepee set up near his old home. He entered, took his bow, arrows, rifle and tomahawk from pegs on the wall and stepped out into the sunshine. He already carried his knife, it was as much a part of his dress as his moccasins.

Bent Feather joined him and together they collected their horses, mounted, rode towards the distant railroad camp.

Bent Feather had been there before. It was he who had caused Lamont so much trouble in his silent vigil. Now he rode to the crest of the skyline and halted his pony, Grave Eagle by his side. Together they sat their mounts and stared down at the activity below.

The railroad camp, like most of its kind, was a huddle of tents and wagons, cut sleepers and cook shacks. A line of them stretched from the further-most point westwards back to the east about twenty to thirty miles apart. Lamont was in charge of this camp and others which he pushed westwards. Even as Bent Feather and Grave Eagle took up their positions a long line of heavily loaded wagons set out westwards, each wagon piled with the shining rails on which the trains were due to run.

The Indians watched as yelling men and straining horses pulled the wagons towards the heart of the Indian territory.

'More white men,' said Bent Feather. 'They go to build another camp towards the setting sun.'

'There are many,' agreed Grave

Eagle. 'They spring like the grass after rain. My heart grows heavy when I count their numbers.'

'The more white men the more scalps to hang in the tepees of the Sioux,' grunted Bent Feather. He stared down towards the camp. 'See, they have Long Knives to protect them.'

'They are children,' said Grave Eagle. 'They are many and all have the rifles which kill from a distance and yet they fear the Sioux.' His eyes shone as he saw the horse lines. 'Look, Bent Feather. It would be great sport to take their horses. They are not guarded and we could steal in at night and take them. None could stop us.'

'Red Arrow has warned that our hands should not be lifted against red man or white,' said Bent Feather. 'I walk with Red Arrow.'

'And I, but there are many horses.'

'Peace.' Bent Feather hid his smile of pride, Grave Eagle was a true Indian. He stiffened as the thin sound of shots echoed from the camp.

'They are shooting at us!' Grave Eagle stared at his father. 'Is this the white man's peace?'

'They are afraid of us.' Bent Feather smiled his contempt at the distant marksmen. The range was far too great for a rifle ball to reach them. He lost his smile as a file of mounted soldiers wheeled from the camp and headed towards the crest on which they stood.

'The Long Knives!'

'We do no wrong,' said Grave Eagle. 'Why should we run?'

'Your words are the words of a warrior,' said Bent Feather. 'But there is a time to fight and a time to run so that we live to fight again. Red Arrow will want to learn of the wagons which have moved westwards. He will not thank us if we stay and fight.'

'We are on the land the white men gave us,' said Grave Eagle. 'Are we women to run without cause?'

Bent Feather hesitated. Alone he would have ridden away and thought nothing of the reason for doing so other than the sport of trying to lead these foolish white men into a foolish chase.

'We follow the words of Red Arrow,' he said. 'Come.'

He dug his heels into his mount and the wiry pony darted away. Grave Eagle, reluctantly, followed but he turned often and his eyes were thoughtful as he stared at the horse lines of the camp. Behind them the cavalry galloped for a few miles before circling and heading back to the camp. Sergeant Watson hated his assignment, it kept his men busy and for no seeming purpose. Fighting he would have enjoyed but this chasing of elusive Indians was annoying. He shook his fist after the two warriors and cursed.

'Take it easy, Sarge,' said a trooper. 'Two more days and we head back to the fort.'

'Them lousy Indians.' The sergeant cursed some more. 'Making us look fools.' He jerked at his reins. 'Let's get back.'

Bent Feather turned when he was

sure that pursuit was over and gestured to his son.

'We ride west,' he said. 'Let us see who is the fastest.'

Grave Eagle nodded and bent low over his mount. He rode as if part of the animal, his lithe body blending with that of the pony as, gripping the saddleless mount, he urged it forward. Beside him Bent Feather rode with practised ease and slowly drew ahead.

They rode until the ponies were tired and then rested the mounts. Night came and they camped, eating cold dried meat and drinking water from a stream. At dawn they mounted and headed westwards again, riding all day and covering the ground at incredible speed. If they had had more than one horse each they would have ridden without pause, changing mounts at regular intervals, eating while riding and covering over a hundred and fifty miles between dawn and sunset. Even as it was they rode like the wind until, attracted by the sound of shots, they halted.

'You ride well,' said Bent Feather.

'I ride as my father taught me.' Grave Eagle listened to the shots. 'White men.'

'They are the buffalo hunters,' said the older warrior, and his face hardened. 'They kill the buffalo for the hides they carry and leave the meat to rot. They kill and kill and soon there will be no buffalo left to feed the Sioux. It is not well that white men should do this thing.'

'They break the treaty again and again,' said Grave Eagle. 'They kill the buffalo and they rob us of our land. It is well that Red Arrow is so patient!'

'Red Arrow walks with the snake, to learn his cunning,' said Bent Feather. 'He walks and speaks soft words to the Chief of the Long Knives. He will hold a great pow-wow with the white man and speak words of sweetness to him. Perhaps the white men will listen to his words and keep the promises they made on the paper. Perhaps they will laugh at

144

Red Arrow and spit on his shadow. If they spit then the Sioux and all those who will ride with us shall beat the drums of war, mix the paint of war, sound the cries of war. Then we shall rise and sweep the white men from our land. So Red Arrow has spoken.'

'Red Arrow is wise. When will he hold pow-wow?'

'After the Great Council. A wise man knows his weapons and Red Arrow is wise.' Bent Feather touched the flanks of his mount. 'Let us see what lies before us.'

He rode towards the sound of the shots.

*　*　*

Mike Wilson, sweat glistening on his forehead, reloaded his shotgun and watched the buffalo before him. He knew the buffalo and knew their habits. For some reason the great beasts did not fear a man on foot but would immediately panic at the sight of a man on horseback. The Indians hunted buffalo from horseback, riding beside the stampeding herds and spearing them as they ran. This was good sport for the Indians and also good training for the young warriors, but the Indians hunted for hides and meat, the white men for money.

An Indian tribe would be satisfied with a few hundred head of buffalo a year, killing only what they needed. The white hunters killed for the sheer slaughter value, shooting and shooting until their guns were hot and the plain was littered with dead beasts. Under the Indian method the buffalo herds were inexhaustible, they replenished themselves by natural increase but they could never restore the lost numbers when attacked by the white hunters. The buffalo, once lords of the prairie, were doomed to virtual extinction.

'How many head?' Mike turned and called to Sam, busy at a second stand a little way from where Mike was standing. The youngster smiled and held up both hands, the fingers outstretched.

'Get back to the others and help work in the camp.' Mike turned and watched the herd before him.

Buffalo did not graze in one great mass. They moved across the prairie in little groups of a score or so, sometimes less, each group parted from the others. The usual system of killing them was for a hunter to set up a stand, usually on a bit of high ground. He would rest his Sharps on its stand and, from a distance of several hundred yards, shoot down the beasts.

A clever hunter could chalk up a kill of maybe a score or more of dead animals before the remainder took fright at the blood-smell and moved off. His danger was almost wholly in the threat of a stampede. The buffalo, if frightened by a man on horseback or by the scent of blood, would suddenly race off at top speed across the prairie. If the hunter happened to be in the line of their charge he had little hope of surviving. For this reason most hunters and all of the camps were put as far from the herds as possible.

Mike had not followed that system. For one thing his camp was pretty close to the herd, though well away from that of other hunters. His weapon was a shotgun, not the cumbersome Sharps .50. He had loaded each shell with a slug of lead weighing over an ounce and to compensate for lack of range-power, he had moved to within a hundred yards of the beasts. His method was simple, effective, and as safe as he could make it.

Once within range he aimed at the heart and dropped the animal nearest to him. Quickly he downed others until one of the surviving beasts lifted his head and snorted as he smelt blood. The trick then was to drop the restless beast before he could spread panic, and then drop others after him until the entire group was either dead or running away from the hunter and his camp.

There were risks, yes, but the tall

man had assessed them and accepted them. The proof of his system was that, in a very short while, he had managed to get his daily kill up to an average of thirty head.

Mike fired and watched the buffalo fall on to its knees. He raised the shotgun again, brought down another animal, then reloaded. He stared at the moving flow of buffalo before him. Despite the continuous slaughter from the white hunters the herds were still so great as to stagger the imagination. More than two million head of buffalo had roamed the prairies before the white men came and, despite the white hunters, many remained. How long they would remain was a matter of conjecture.

Sam came from the camp, his skinning knife in his hand.

'Ready to call it a day?'

'Might as well.' Mike lowered his shotgun. 'No sense in killing more than we can skin.' He glanced at the sky. 'Let's get busy and stretch out the hides. Zeke back yet?'

'Just coming.' Sam led the way back to the camp. Old Abel and Jud were red to the elbows from buffalo blood and the place reeked of freshly killed meat. All the men were tired from gruelling labour; skinning the great animals was hard work, but the pile of stretched and salted hides waiting transportation spoke of the success of the venture.

Abel grinned as Mike approached and leaned back from his labours.

'Man, I sure didn't think that skinning buffalo was such hard work.'

'Take a break.' Mike squinted towards the approaching wagon. 'When Zeke arrives we'll load up and change teams. Jud can run this load down to the buffalo camp and sell the hides to the buyers. Abel can take the other wagon and deliver some of the meat to the rail-camp. While you're away, Sam, Jud and I will get some more hides ready.'

'Don't you ever rest?' The old man wiped his hands and felt for a plug of chewing tobacco. 'How long you going to keep this pace up?'

'As long as we can. The buffalo are always on the move which means that we've got to follow them. The further we follow them the further we'll have to drag the meat to the rail-camp. That's a paying contract at the moment and we don't want to lose it.' He stared at the horizon. 'And there's another reason.'

'Which is?'

'Indians.' Mike pointed. 'See? There are a couple of them up there watching us.'

'So what?' Abel shrugged. 'They can't hurt us, be fools to try. Forget them.'

'They're Sioux,' said Mike slowly. 'They think that this is their land and these are their buffalo. Without the buffalo they will starve. If I was an Indian I think that I'd be tempted to do something about it.'

'What can they do?' The old man snorted. 'Hell, I ain't afraid of no Indians.' He grinned up at his son as the wagon drew to a halt beside the camp. 'Hi, Zeke, have any trouble?'

'Not a scrap.' The young man jumped down from the wagon. 'Why, expecting any?'

'Mike's seen a couple of Indians.' Abel jerked his thumb towards the horizon. 'He reckons they ain't friendly.'

'I didn't see them.' Zeke helped himself to coffee. 'Lamont sent word that he wants to see you, Mike. Said something about the new fort going through and wants you to take charge of scouting or something like that.' He looked anxious. 'I hope that he don't talk you into leaving us.'

'He won't,' said Mike. He stared towards the horizon, his face anxious.

'Something bothering you?' Zeke squinted over the prairie.

'Those Indians. I can't see them any more.' Mike shrugged. 'Well, you never can tell with Indians. I . . . ' He broke off, his eyes narrowed as he stared towards the east.

'Something?' Sam stepped beside the

tall man. Mike gestured for silence.

'Horses,' said Sam. 'Coming fast.'

'It's those damned Indians,' said Zeke. 'They're riding straight towards us! He shook his head. 'The crazy sons-of-guns! What do they think they're doing?'

'Where?' Mike jumped on to the wagon, lifted himself to the canopy and shaded his eyes. Beyond the sea of brown-backed buffalo Bent Feather and Grave Eagle were riding, both stretched along the backs of their ponies and heading directly towards the herd. Even as Mike watched they rose upright and, as if coming from one throat, the shrilling war whoop of the Sioux rang over the prairie.

Mike jumped from the wagon.

'Get to your horse,' he snapped. 'Quick!' He began running towards the horses tethered well away from the herd. Sam stared after him, looked at the old man, then followed Mike.

'Wait!' Abel yelled after the tall man. 'What's the hurry?'

'Stampede,' shouted Mike. 'Get to your horses fast!'

'They aren't moving,' gasped Sam as he drew level with the tall man. 'They don't understand.'

'I've warned them and told them a dozen times.' Mike speeded up as the bellowing from the startled buffalo mounted higher. 'When the herd starts to stampede you've got to get away from them, fast! Those damn Indians are deliberately turning the herd against us. Unless we get moving we won't stand a chance!'

He reached the horses, freed them, swung into his saddle. Gripping the reins of the spare horses he spurred back towards the camp. Old man Abel, his mouth hanging open in surprise and shock, looked up as Mike thundered to a halt. 'Mount,' snapped the tall man. 'Get on a horse, your sons as well, and get moving!'

'Why?' Abel swallowed. 'What's the hurry?'

'Listen.' Mike lifted his hand. From

the herd came a bellowing and then, like the muted roll of drums, a dull thunder as ten thousand hooves hit the sundried ground of the prairie.

'Stampede,' shouted Mike. 'Ride for your lives!'

'The money!' Abel turned to the camp. 'I've got all my money in the tent. And guns, all my stuff's in there.'

'Fool!' Mike craned his head towards the oncoming buffalo. 'Ride!' He spurred his mount and rode towards where Sam was waiting. He rode like a madman, racing against time and certain destruction. Behind him Abel and his sons, after a fatal moment's delay, grabbed at the horses and swung into the saddles.

They were too late.

Almost three thousand buffalo charged towards the camp. Each animal weighed almost a quarter of a ton and nothing could stand before them. The wagons were smashed to matchwood, the tents trodden into the ground, the cooking utensils, the guns, the food, everything, was tramped and ground beneath the sharp hooves.

The three men didn't stand a chance.

They tried but their delay had been fatal. They rode as best they could but their horses were knocked from under them and, when the buffalo had passed, nothing remained of old man Abel and his sons.

Mike pulled rein when he was sure that he and Sam were beyond danger and, as he started at the place where the camp had stood, his face was hard.

'It was deliberate,' said Sam. 'Those two Indians knew what would happen if they charged the buffalo on horseback. They killed those men and they tried to kill us.'

'It was deliberate,' said Mike. 'But can we prove it? Would it matter if we could? The Indians own this land and they are supposed to own the buffalo. Those two were quick to take a chance. They knew we couldn't attack them or they attack us. So they turned the buffalo against us.' He shrugged. 'Clever.'

'Clever?' Sam looked ill. 'Is that what you call it?'

'In war anything is clever if it helps you to win,' said Mike. He touched spurs to the flanks of his horse. 'Let's go see what Lamont wants.'

He didn't look back.

8

Before the Council tepee a great fire blazed. Around it sat the elders and the great warriors of the Sioux. With them, dressed in their ceremonial robes, sat the Chiefs of the Cheyenne, the Comanche, and the Apache from the New Mexico border. They sat as befitted great warriors, their faces impassive, their eyes glinting in the dancing firelight.

The pipe of peace had been passed and all had puffed smoke towards the four corners of the earth, the sky and the ground. The Shaman had danced the dance of good fortune and the dance of friendship. Now all men sat and waited for the words of Red Arrow, Chief of the Sioux. He rose, tall and splendid in his robes, his aged but intelligent face stern as he stared around the circle. Not often was there a

Great Council of all the chiefs of all the tribes. Among the tribes of one people there had been such councils, but these were hereditary enemies, tribes who had fought each other for generations. The fact that they had agreed to smoke the pipe of peace together showed how much they respected Red Arrow.

'If a man wishes to move a heavy tree,' said the Chief, 'And that tree is too great for him to lift, it is wise for him to call his brothers to help him. But it would be foolish for those brothers to pull, one against the other, or for some to sit on the tree while the others lifted, or for them to fight among themselves instead of working together.' He paused, looking at the circle of faces. 'It is wise for two hunters to trap a deer and slay it. It is foolish for those hunters to quarrel over who is to have the skin while the sly wolf steals their game.'

'It is foolish for men to talk of what they will do with the buffalo they have yet to catch.' Little Bear, Chief of the

Comanche, looked around the circle as he spoke. 'My brother Red Arrow speaks strong words. Are there any who does not understand what he says?'

'We of the Apache understand,' said a lank-haired warrior. The Apache did not take scalps and wore their hair differently to the Sioux but they were skilled and cunning in war. Najaji, who spoke for Cochise, Chief of the Apache, stared at Red Arrow. 'We of the south have long learned this lesson. If we are to fight the white men then we must be as brothers. The White Eyes are as the sands of the desert and we are few. To waste our strength fighting ourselves is to die by our own hand.'

Grunts, deep-chested gutturals greeted his words. The Great Council was in full agreement.

'Hear my words.' said Red Arrow. 'You have heard and know the treaty I signed with the Long Knives. They gave me a paper which said that this land was the land of the Sioux. They said that no white man would enter our land. This land was to be ours for all time.' He paused. 'They lied.'

'The white man always lie,' said Running Dog, Chief of the Cheyenne. 'They speak with forked tongues.'

'We kept the peace,' said Red Arrow. 'We stayed our young warriors when they would have stolen the horses of the white men. We held our hand when the wagons of the white men moved across our plains. We moved not when the hunters began to kill the buffalo and take away our food. We did nothing when the shining rail pushed into the land which the white men had given us. This was bad but we did nothing.

'We sat and watched as the shining rails grew and grew, as the buffalo died, as men and more men took our game and searched for the yellow iron. But all things must stop and each has a limit beyond which he will not go. The Sioux are a patient people but our patience is not limitless. Still we held our hand for peace is dear to our hearts and we would not waste our young warriors in battle against the Long Knives. But now we must act. For the Long Knives are building a fort where no fort should be. The camps of the men who lay the shining rails are stretched from the east to the west. This land is no longer the land of the Sioux.'

'It is a story often repeated,' said Najaji. 'The Apache has been fighting the white men for many years.'

'Hear my words,' said Red Arrow. 'Yesterday we were enemies, now we are as brothers. We of the Sioux ask your aid. Alone we shall fight the white men and alone we shall die. This is a thing that shall be done. But as we die so you also will die. What is happening to the Sioux will happen to the Cheyenne and the Comanche, it is already happening to the Apache as you all know. Now is the time for us to forget that once we fought against each other. Now is the time to remember that we are red man against white. All red men against all white men.'

His voice rang on, pressing home

point after point, stressing the need for co-operation and detailing his plan as to attack if his pow-wow should prove unsatisfactory. What he proposed was, to a white man, simplicity itself. He proposed that all the tribes should gather their fighting men and send them out as a strong force instead of as a handful of scattered war parties. To a white man the logic would have been obvious, the only thing to do, but to an Indian the task was almost impossible.

Cochise of the Apache had done it. He had achieved the impossible in uniting the various tribes of the Apache and persuading them to follow his leadership. Because of that he had managed to gain complete control of the southem deserts to an extent almost impossible for anyone not there to realize. Not even the mail could be carried, no supplies for the troops, no wagon trains from east to west or from west to east. No white man could cross Apache Pass. If he tried it then a humming arrow would speed from behind a boulder or a rifle send lead through his skull. Cochise, because he had managed to persuade the Indians to accept his discipline, had shown what the Indians could do in their own country.

Red Arrow hoped to do the same.

For a lesser warrior to have tried it would have been for him to earn contempt. Only the high regard in which he was held had persuaded the Chiefs to attend the Great Council. His logic was understood by all. The need to repulse the white man was accepted. Running Dog voiced the first objection.

'Winter comes,' he said. 'If the warriors are fighting the white men, then who will feed the women and children, the old and the weak?'

'We will fight,' said Little Bear. 'But my brother of the Cheyenne speaks strong words. How long will it take to sweep the white men from the land of the Sioux?'

'They will never be swept away,' said Najaji. He rose and stared around the circle. 'Hear my words, the words of Cochise through the mouth of Najaji, his ananda, his brother in blood. Hear the words of Cochise the Great Chief of the Apache.' His voice deepened almost as if it was indeed the voice of Cochise instead of merely his relayed message.

'To think of sweeping the white men into the sea is to think like a child. To think of earning their respect is to think like a warrior. The Sioux cannot put back the sun. They are not as their fathers or their fathers before them. They are warriors but they are Indians. They think Indian thoughts and live Indian ways. They are not white men and cannot fight like white men. They are as children in the dark for they know little of white man's war. I, Cochise, will tell them what must be done.

'The white men have broken the treaty and will tread the Sioux into the dirt. Let the Sioux fight but let them make sure that they fight only when all else fails. Let them tell the white men this. Then, when they fight, let them strike hard and with all their strength. Let all who hate the white men fight as one. Let the white man ask for peace and offer a new treaty. Let the Sioux accept their terms.'

Najaji paused and shook himself. 'So are the words of Cochise.'

A sigh ran around the circle, a mutter of agreement with what had been said. Red Arrow held up his hand.

'Cochise is a great warrior, skilled and wise in the ways of war. Yet Apache land is not Sioux land.'

'Our quarrel is the same quarrel,' pointed out Najaji. 'We too have trusted the White Eyes and have had them spit in our face.'

'That is true,' admitted Red Arrow. He stared around the circle. 'This I ask. Let us bury the hatchet and become as brothers against the white men. As Cochise says so we will do. In two days I go to the new fort to talk with the Chief of the Long Knives. If he burns his walls and stops the shining rails then we shall live in peace. If he does not do this, or lifts his hand against us, then we shall ride the warpath. Is it agreed?'

For a moment the Chiefs looked at each other.

'I walk with Red Arrow.' Running Dog rose to his feet. 'I bury the hatchet.' He took a tomahawk from his belt and threw it into a shallow hole in the ground.

'I walk with Red Arrow.' Little Bear rose and did the same. One after the other the lesser Chiefs and assembled warriors rose and repeated their allegiance. When all had spoken the Shaman danced forward, rattling his gourd.

'In this grave the hatchets of enemies lie,' he said. 'Let them be covered from the sight of men.' He kicked dirt over the weapons. 'Until such time as these hatchets are uncovered to the light of day there shall be no enemies between us.'

'It is well,' said Najaji. 'But remember

the words of Cochise. Can a man catch all the rain?'

'I have taken the words of Cochise to my heart.' Red Arrow lifted his arms. 'Tomorrow is the day of decision. To your tribes then, oh, my brothers. If Manitou has decreed war then the drums shall beat and all the world shall learn that the Sioux are mixing their war paint. When you hear the drums send out your warriors. Kill. Burn. Slay. Spare none.'

He stood for a moment and then relaxed. Slowly he moved to his tepee while, all around him, the visitors walked towards their ponies. They would ride fast and hard and yet, so great were the distances some had to cover, they would not reach their tribes until after the pow-wow. It could well be that they would only arrive with the relayed pounding of the war drums to signal both their arrival and the time of war. Lame Horse, the Shaman, watched them go and then went in to join his brother.

'Much blood will be spilt, my brother,' he said. 'I do not think that there will be peace.'

'Then there will be war.' Red Arrow stared through the open flap of his tepee towards the dying fire. 'I had left the Great Council to this late hour so that the white men would not guess what we plan. I have sent word to the Chief of the Long Knives that in two days I shall be at the new fort. If he desires peace then he will meet me there.'

'And if he is not?'

'Then there will be war.' Red Arrow glanced towards the big drum standing by the Council tepee. It was half the height of a man, covered with taut deerskin and painted red and black. It was the great war drum of the Sioux.

Lame Horse followed his glance.

'It is long since the war drum beat for the Sioux,' he said. 'I had hoped that it would not beat again.'

'You are not a warrior,' said Red Arrow, but he spoke without malice.

169

'You are a man of peace as befits one who talks with the spirits. But can there be a peaceful way for the Sioux?'

'There could be.' Lame Horse hesitated. 'I spoke with Najaji before the Council. It seems that the white men are offering land to tribes who wish to take them. They give food and blankets and seeds and cattle. The reservations are filled with many tribes.'

'We have spoken of this before.' said Red Arrow. 'The Sioux are not those who grow crops or tend cattle. Such work is the work of women.'

'The white men grow crops and tend cattle,' reminded Lame Horse. 'Are they women?'

'Their ways are not our ways.'

'We could learn their ways.' Lame Horse looked at his brother. 'I am not a warrior, Red Arrow, and it could be that I see things in a different light to one who wears many coup. But I see that we are doomed. The buffalo are going and what shall we do when they are gone? Our warriors are dying and many are slave to the fire-water they buy from the traders. Our squaws wail with their hunger each winter and many children die. Is it not better to save a part than lose the whole?'

'Can the eagle be caged?' Red Arrow stared at the Shaman. 'I too have heard tales of these reservations. Poor land without game and without buffalo. We would sit and grow grass like the white men or raise cattle. Where would our young warriors gain their coup? How would we teach them to live in the ways of their fathers? Without war how could they pass from men into warriors and wear their paint? The old ways are good ways, Lame Horse. Let us not talk more of this.'

'Yesterday was a good day,' said the Shaman. 'But it is gone for ever. Gone as the old days are gone. To live in the past is to grow old. Are you so old, Red Arrow?'

'I am perhaps too old to wish to learn new ways,' said the Chief sternly. 'I did not take you for a friend of the white man.'

'I am the friend of all men,' said the Shaman. 'We all have spirits, we all bleed, we all die. The white squaws feel sorrow as the red squaws do. The white warriors die as the red ones do.' He rose and stepped to the flap of the tepee. 'This is a big land. Red Arrow, too big for a few men when many go hungry.'

'Are we to be slaves because we are few and they are many?' Red Arrow shivered as if at a sudden chill. 'You speak good words, I know, but they weigh heavy on my heart. To live in peace is my desire for I know, as well as you, that war can lead only to our death. But to gain that peace we must fight. For the white eyes are like the Indians in that they do not respect an unworthy foe. Let us prove ourselves and then, as Cochise has advised, we will sign a new treaty.'

'And then, when the treaty is broken as the others have been?'

'Who knows? Perhaps we will fight again.'

'And more warriors will die.' Lame Horse nodded. 'And so it will go on until the last Sioux is beaten. I do not think that time will be far.'

'Leave me.' Red Arrow pointed towards the flap of the tepee. 'You turn my strength into water with your words.'

'I go.' Lame Horse stepped from the tepee and walked slowly down the village. He passed the squaws sitting outside their tepees busy sewing or gnawing at hides to make them soft. He passed warriors testing the fastenings of arrow and lance heads, fitting fresh feathers on the wickedly barbed war arrows used instead of the unbarbed ones reserved for game. A few children were playing with miniature bow and arrows and a couple of striplings were wrestling to the watchful appraisal of several warriors.

Beyond the village the Shaman halted and stared up at the sky. The night was clear, the moon a thin crescent low on the horizon and, high above, the stars shone and glittered as if they were a double handful of jewels cast by some cosmic jeweller against the black velvet of night. For a long while the Shaman stared at them, tracing in the constellations the legends of his people and looking, perhaps, for some sign as to the future of the Sioux.

Then he shivered and returned to his tepee.

9

Grave Eagle was enjoying himself. He lay flat on his stomach and stared towards the railroad camp just ahead. It was night but several fires and lanterns threw a ruby light over the scene. Work had finished for the day, the evening meal had been eaten, and the tough, hard-bitten railway workers were enjoying themselves. A group of them formed a circle and watched a pair of champions slug it out with bare knuckles. Most of the onlookers had laid bets on the outcome and their shouts echoed over the prairie.

The noise was quite loud enough to drown any sound the young warrior may have made.

But he made no noise. Like a snake he rippled forward over the sun-burnt grass, his copper skin gleaming with grease, his weapons at his waist. His eyes glittered as he moved and he thrilled to the excitement of danger. At other times he could have been after scalps but now his mission was more peaceful.

He was going to steal horses.

Ever since the time when he had first looked down on the camp he had wanted to test his skill against the guards of the white men. The horse lines were some little distance from the camp, the animals penned in a rough corral without any proper guards. To an Indian it was an open invitation to steal the animals.

Grave Eagle didn't worry about the words of Red Arrow, the big pow-wow which was due to be held at the new fort or the peace which the Indian tried to keep. Like all Indian children he had never known discipline or physical punishment. Like all Indian children he had done exactly as he wanted to do all his life. The system under which the Indians reared their children gave to each member of the tribe an incredibly strong sense of security and a stoical acceptance of their fate. They were individuals from the moment of their birth and were loved and cherished as no white child had ever been. No Indian could understand why the white men beat their children and the sight of a man beating his child for some slight fault filled the red man with contempt and disgust.

The system bred strong individuals who belonged to the family of the tribe and owned allegiance to the tribe alone. But it also bred individuals who saw no reason for not doing what they wanted to do when they wanted. Red Arrow could not command, he could only ask. He had said that no hand was to be lifted against the white man and Grave Eagle agreed with the Great Chief. But horse stealing was different and Grave Eagle was eager to prove himself a warrior.

So he wriggled towards the horse lines of the railcamp and felt no sense of shame or guilt or anything but the thrill of the chase.

Shame or guilt, to an Indian, were emotions so rarely felt that, when they were, he would ask his friends to kill him to end his misery. An Indian was his own law and his own master. He lived by custom, not command.

Grave Eagle smiled as he smelt the scent of horses. The white men were stupid fools to leave them so weakly guarded. He could imagine Bent Feather's smile of pride when he returned to the village with the stolen mounts and there would be rejoicing at his exploit. Great Chiefs were men who took many risks and provided the village with much food and the spoils of war. Grave Eagle, though young, was ambitious. He too wanted to sit in the Council and have men listen to his words with respect.

He hunched closer to the dim silhouettes of the horses.

Towards the other end of the camp, sitting in a tent lit by an odorous lantern, Major Lamont sat and talked to Mike.

'This pow-wow,' said the railroad boss. 'You think anything will come of it?'

'Maybe.' Mike stretched his booted legs and drew at his cigar. He had ridden hard that day and felt tired. Since the time when the stampede had wiped out his hopes of a successful buffalo hunt he and Sam had worked at the site of the new fort, supplying the troops with meat and game.

'I don't like it,' said Lamont. 'I've heard tell of what that crazy Indian Red Arrow wants. He wants to stop the railroad and tear down the fort.' He shrugged and reached towards a bottle of whiskey. 'He's wasting his time.'

'Isn't that up to General Clarke?'

'The General's got to obey orders,' said Lamont. 'He's here to protect the citizens. If the Indians attack the railroad then he'll have to send his cavalry against them. Talk won't alter that.' He lifted the bottle. 'Drink?'

'Sure.' Mike took the glass and sipped the raw spirit. 'I half-promised to ride over to the fort for the pow-wow,' he said. 'I left Sam with the General.'

'The youngster?' Lamont shrugged. 'I know that he's your partner and I've seen him in action but can he handle himself in an Indian war?'

'I think so.' Mike emptied and refilled his glass. 'What makes you so certain that there will be a war?'

'There's got to be.' Lamont was cynical. 'We can't develop this country while the Indians are riding around killing and stealing. While the buffalo roam the prairies we can't stop them but, once we cut off their food supply, then they'll have to come to heel. Damn it! Why can't they see sense? We're too big for them and they don't stand a chance. If they went into reservations our troubles would be over.'

'They're in a reservation now,' pointed out Mike. 'The Indian Bureau granted them this land. The Indian

Nations is supposed to be for the benefit of the red man. Now we've broken our treaty with them. You think that they'll trust us after this?'

'Who cares?' Lamont took another drink. 'The only good Indian is a dead one. The quicker there are only good Indians left the better I'll like it.' He cocked his head at a burst of cheering from outside. 'The boys are having themselves a time.'

'They earn it,' said Mike. 'How's the meat supply?'

'You should know. I've signed on a couple more hunters and they manage to keep us fed.' Lamont leaned forward. 'Thought about that proposition?'

'Some.' Mike took the cigar from his mouth and looked at it. 'You're set on pushing this railroad through no matter what the cost?'

'I am. If the General tries to stop me then he'll be broken. If the Indians try to stop me then they'll find they are wasting their time.' Lamont became urgent. 'Look at it this way, Mike. We're

181

going to have a showdown, that's obvious. Well, why wait for the Indians to hit first? Let's take a few men and ride up to their village. We can cut them down and burn the tepees and wipe out the threat to the railroad. Once we do that, show the red devils that we mean business, then they'll leave us alone.'

'Maybe.'

'All right.' Lamont rose to his feet. 'So you don't see things my way. Why?'

'I don't reckon it's wise to stir up a hornets' nest,' said Mike. 'We're in Indian territory, deep in the heart of the Nations. You try stamping out a village and you'll raise every Indian on the warpath. The camps are isolated and undefended. The men are armed, sure, but how long do you think they could hold out? If you ride against a village you'll start something you won't be able to finish.'

'I think I will,' said Lamont. 'The railway has been completed up to Fort Hemridge. That means that the soldiers can get there fast from back east. In fact there is a big garrison at the fort now.' He grinned. 'I've got a few brains, Wilson, and I've got backing. I told you this railroad was going through. Those soldiers back at Fort Hemridge are there to stamp out any uprising. If the Indians get any bright ideas about attacking the railroad they'll find out that they've bitten off more than they can chew.'

'Clever,' said Mike. 'Very clever.'

'Just good sense.'

'Your sort of sense.'

'What do you mean?'

'I mean just this. You are determined to push ahead and lay steel. All right, that's your job, but do you have to be in so much of a hurry?'

'The job's got to be done and I'm the man to do it.'

'You're a dog, Lamont,' said Mike, and now he was no longer smiling. 'You want an Indian war and, if you can't get one, then you'll start one all on your own. You know that once the Indians rise up the cavalry will have to crush them. That'll leave you sitting pretty. You can lay steel where and how you like, take the Indians' land, stake out claims and . . . ' He paused. 'Claims, so that's it.'

'What are you talking about?' Lamont wet his lips. 'You don't know what you're saying.'

'No?' Mike shrugged. 'I think that I do. You get all sorts hanging around your camp, don't you, Lamont?'

'What of it?'

'Traders and prospectors and gamblers. You've even grub-staked a few prospectors, haven't you?'

'What of it?'

'I'm thinking.' Mike narrowed his eyes, then nodded. 'The Indian Nations is pretty big and there's a lot of it we don't know all about yet. The way things are we won't know about it for a long time. But supposing that a big strike of gold had been found deep in Indian territory? Suppose that you knew just where this strike was and that you couldn't register it because you had no chance to grab the claim? He nodded again. 'Am I making sense, Lamont?'

'Are you?' The big man shrugged. 'Seems like a lot of hot air to me.'

'Maybe, and yet it all makes sense.' Mike snorted, then grinned. 'I said you were a dog, Lamont. I take it back. You're first brother to a snake.'

'Watch it Wilson,' warned Lamont. 'I don't go for that kind of talk.'

'Don't you?' Mike shrugged. 'I meant it as a compliment. An Indian would take it that way.'

'I'm not an Indian.'

'No,' said the tall man thoughtfully. 'An Indian wouldn't think the way you do.' He smiled. 'You're clever, Lamont. I've got to admit that. All the time I figured that you just wanted to push ahead laying steel. Everyone thought that, even the General. But all the time you've been using the railroad to cover your real aims. There's gold in the Indian territory and you know where it is. You know that, if the Indians go on the warpath, they'll be wiped out and the Nations thrown open for settlement. You figure on starting an Indian war so that you can get in and grab the pay dirt. Right?'

'You're doing the talking,' said Lamont.

'I'm right,' said Mike. He shook his head. 'It's a nice plan but it won't work.'

'Why not?'

'So you admit that I'm right?'

'I admit nothing!' snapped Lamont. 'But, just supposing that you had the right idea, why wouldn't the plan work?'

'You don't know the country,' said Mike. 'You don't know the Indians. You don't know much about what you're doing. You need a partner.'

'So that's it.' Lamont grinned with relief. 'So you want to cut in.'

'Why not?'

'I figured you for an Indian lover,' said Lamont. 'I didn't think that you'd see things my way.'

'I can see both sides to a question,' said Mike. 'I also like money, lots of money, the more money the better.' His face darkened. 'I have a good use for it.'

'We all have,' said Lamont. He hesitated, wondering whether to trust the tall man and, at the same time, wondering how to get rid of him should he prove troublesome. Mike stared at him, knowing just what he was thinking. Lamont wasn't to be trusted. He was a man who would cheerfully set the west ablaze with Indian war to grab the gold he knew was waiting for the right man.

'Well?'

'Let me think about it,' said Lamont. 'I'm not admitting anything, my sole concern is to get the railroad finished but if . . . ' He paused.

'If by any chance you should need a good, reliable, trustworthy man,' said Mike sarcastically, 'you know where to come.' He dropped his cigar, trod on it, and headed for the flap of the tent. 'Be cautious, Lamont, but remember this.

Time is running out so don't leave things too long. I've a mind to do a little prospecting myself.'

'Why not?' said Lamont. 'It's healthy exercise.' Together they stepped out into the night.

The fight was over and the loser, battered and bloody, had been carried to his tent. The winner, in very little better condition, was being carried about the camp on the shoulders of the men who had backed him.

They were a rough, hard-bitten crew, all carrying guns and knives for defence against the Indians but rarely used in their private quarrels. Gunplay was not popular but fist fighting was. Arguments were settled with bare knuckles and iron-tipped boots. Sometimes a pair of visiting buffalo hunters would fight a duel with their Sharps rifles, setting them up at a distance of about a hundred yards and firing until one was hit. Rarely was more than one shot required, they were men who depended on their marksmanship for a living, and the impact of one of the big bullets was always fatal.

A whiskey wagon had arrived at the camp at sundown and it was thronged by a jostling group of men. Mike and Lamont shoved their way forward to the tail of the wagon where a stunted character was busy taking money and filling pannikins and tin cups from his barrels.

'Step right up,' he yelled. 'Pay your money and get a big drink of the finest whiskey this side of the Allegenhies.' He recognized Lamont and handed him a tin cup. 'On the house, boss. On the house.'

'You have it.' Lamont handed the cup to Mike. 'It's too raw for me.'

'Thanks.' Mike tasted the brew, held it in his mouth for a moment, then spat it out. The crude whiskey burned and had a kick like a mule. The railroad man and buffalo hunters judged their whiskey by the kick and red pepper, tabasco, curry powder, creosote and other ingredients were mixed with the raw alcohol and burnt sugar for flavouring.

'Like it?' Lamont looked at the tall man. Mike looked thoughtful. He tasted the whiskey again, smelt it then tossed it aside.

'You,' he said to the whiskey pedlar. 'What you put in this stuff?'

'Only the best,' said the man. He grinned down from the top of his wagon. 'Good, ain't it?'

'It's poison.' Mike looked at Lamont. 'If you want to get these men working tomorrow you'll run this wagon out of the camp.'

'You can't do that!' yelled the pedlar. Like most of his kind he was a transient merchant, filling his barrels with the nearest and cheapest approach to whiskey he could think of, making sure that it burned and had a kick, then driving from camp to camp selling his wares. The whiskey pedlars were a part of prairie life and regular sights at railroad and buffalo camps. Most sold drinkable whiskey, raw but basically harmless. Some took the opportunity for a quick profit, selling near-poison and making a fast circle of the camps before selling their rot-gut to the Indians.

'I can if I want to,' said Lamont, bridling at the challenge. 'Let me taste that stuff.'

'Sure.' The pedlar filled a cup, hiding it with his body. Here.'

Lamont sipped it, looked surprised, took a longer drink.

'Nothing wrong with this.'

'Let me taste it.' Mike sipped, rolled the brew around his mouth, then spat it out. 'I thought so. He's got a special barrel.' He snatched a pannikin from a railroad worker. 'Try this.'

'Poison.' Lamont coughed and spat. 'What's he put in it?'

'Only he knows that but one thing's for sure. If the men get drunk on it they won't be able to move tomorrow.'

With a quick spring Mike jumped on to the wagon and uplifted the barrel from which the pedlar was serving.

Taking the Colt from the holster at his side he made sure that an empty chamber was under the hammer, reversed the gun, and beat in the head of the barrel with the heavy butt. The pedlar yelled in protest but Mike ignored him. He was staring into the barrel.

'What's this?'

'It strengthens the brew,' said the pedlar. 'Gives it bite.'

'What is it?' called out Lamont. 'What have you found?'

'This.' Mike dipped into the barrel and lifted out a handful of long, slender objects. 'Snakes! Dead rattlesnakes! No wonder it tasted like poison.'

'They don't do any hurt,' yelled the pedlar. He swallowed, his face white. 'It gives the whiskey more body. I always put a couple of rattlers into each barrel. I always have done and haven't had a complaint yet.'

'You're getting one now,' snapped Lamont. 'Get out of camp.' He looked around at the workers, all of whom had heard what had been said. 'We don't want his poison, do we?' yelled Lamont. 'We don't want to drink snake-juice.'

Secretly he was pleased at the discovery. The railroad workers were hard to handle at the best of times and with a night-long drinking session behind them they would be unmanageable in the morning. Normally Lamont would have been reluctant to order a whiskey pedlar from the camp, to have done so would have been to arouse the men against him, but this time he would have no trouble.

'The swine.' yelled a burly plate-layer. 'Selling us poison. He should be lynched.'

'Dip him in his own barrels,' shouted a man. 'Pickle him like he does the snakes.'

A yell answered the suggestion and the pedlar, his face white, clutched at Mike.

'Save me,' he whimpered. 'They'll lynch me for sure less you stop them.'

'Get out of here,' snapped Mike. 'Fast!'

'I'm going.' The pedlar jumped down to his driving seat, snatched up the reins and yelled at the horses. They shifted but couldn't move, the press of angry men around them was too great. Mike lifted his Colt, thumbed back the hammer and fired into the air. The sudden report brought a momentary silence.

'Hold it!' Mike lowered the gun. 'Let this coyote get away from here. If he comes back we'll make a fire of his wagon and roast him over it.'

'Let's do it now,' yelled a man.

'What for, we've plenty of meat, haven't we?' Mike waited for the laughter to die. 'All right, we've had our fun, now let go the horses and let him go.'

'No!' The man who had shouted before clutched at the wagon. 'Let's string him up.'

'You heard what I said!' shouted Mike. He raised his gun and sent lead blasting into the air. 'Now listen. This man is going to ride from camp and you aren't going to stop him.' He stared down at the sea of faces surrounding the wagon. 'Just to make sure of that I'm going to ride with him to the edge of the camp.' He levelled the long-barrelled Colt. 'If anyone has other ideas he'd better forget them. Understand?'

'He won't shoot,' yelled the man. 'If he does we'll string him up too. Come on lads, what are you waiting for?'

A growling tide of angry men moved towards the wagon.

Mike stared at them, the gun steady in his hand, knowing that he could kill several but that, inevitably, he would be overpowered. He hesitated, the long barrel of the Colt drifting from one man to the other. He was reluctant to shoot but knew that he would finish what he had started. Beside him the whiskey pedlar cringed with fear.

'Come down, Wilson,' called Lamont. 'What's that man to you?'

'He's leaving here under his own power,' said Mike grimly. He stood, tall and hard in the light of the fires, the gun in his hand a shining finger of menace. The crowd surged around the wagon, eager to vent their rage on the hapless pedlar but reluctant to face the deadly fire of the Colt. For a moment action hung in the balance and, in the way of crowds, a silence fell.

In that silence the scream of a man sounded like the shrieking of a devil.

Together with that scream came another sound, a sound once heard never forgotten.

The war whoop of the Sioux.

10

At first everything was too easy. Grave Eagle had managed to wriggle directly up to the horses and was pondering on which to take. From the far end of the camp a roaring noise drowned any slight sound and the horse lines seemed deserted. The young warrior wriggled closer then, shielded by the horses, rose up among them like a slim copper shadow.

He had come prepared. In his hands he held halters made of rawhide soaked in salt and he let the horses smell them, licking at the leather, eager for the salt with which they were covered. While they nuzzled the halters he spoke to them, letting them become accustomed to the scent of his body and his presence. The great danger when stealing horses was that they would take fright and bolt, whinneying and attracting attention.

For long minutes Grave Eagle talked to the horses and moved softly among them. He was searching for the best mounts, knowing that he could not take them all. Gently he threw a halter over the head of a big gelding, stroking it and soothing its fears. The gelding ready, he chose a bay, then a smaller pony with splotches so loved by the Indians. To them a paint pony was the best of all.

The three horses fitted with halters, Grave Eagle was ready to go. Gently he led them towards the gate of the corral, lifted the rough bars and led them out. Carefully he replaced the bars behind him, knowing that an open gate would arouse immediate suspicion but that a casual glance, would not reveal the missing horses.

Outside the corral he moved a little faster, watching for guards and moving like a shadow. He began to breathe easier as he increased the distance from the corral. The white men were indeed fools that they should guard their horses so badly.

Grave Eagle was young, impatient, and lacked the full cunning of an older warrior. Even at that it was sheer bad luck that one of the horses should stumble, kick hard against a stone and send sparks flying from the metal shoe it wore.

It was even worse luck that the old man detailed as horse tender should have looked in that direction at exactly that time.

'Who's there?' Old man Johnson rose from where he had been sitting with his Winchester across his knees. He raised the rifle as he peered into the darkness. 'Hold it or I fire!'

It was bluff, but Grave Eagle didn't know that. The old man could see nothing but the dim shapes of the horses and, for all he knew, they belonged to riders coming to camp. But such riders would have called out, the silence made him even more suspicious.

'I can see you.' he yelled. 'Halt or I'll shoot!'

Grave Eagle halted. He had seen the effects of rifle bullets and knew that the whites' guns could shoot far and accurately. He himself had no gun, just his knife and tomahawk. He had spotted the guard and, in normal times, would have silenced him before stealing the horses. But there was peace between red man and white and Grave Eagle had resisted the temptation to collect an easy scalp.

'I'm coming after you,' said Old Johnson. He stepped forward, the rifle at the ready. In the distant glow of the camp fires he could see the shapes of the horses and, as he came closer, recognized them as belonging to the corral. As yet he had not seen the Indian.

Grave Eagle stood for a moment in indecision. He could run and leave the horses and would be safe. But he had set his heart on stealing them and it galled him to have come so near success. He had dreamed of his triumphal return to the village with the horses and the admiration which the older warriors would give him. Horses, to the Indians, are wealth, the only wealth they knew. With horses a warrior could buy a squaw and the more horses he had the wider his choice of squaws would be. To yield now, just because of an old man, was more than he could stomach.

Softly he dropped to the ground, merging into the shadows. Silently he crept towards the old man, his tomahawk ready in his hand. Killing, to Grave Eagle was nothing, it was just a part of the game of war. He knew that the guard would shoot him without question but, even as he raised the tomahawk, he remembered the words of Red Arrow.

There was peace between red man and white. He must not kill the white man.

He grunted with disappointment and, when he grunted, old man

Johnson turned and stared directly into his face.

The shock, as much as anything else, tore the scream from the old man's lips. He expected immediate death, thought of an attack, anything, and his shriek was as much to give warning as an expression of his own fear. He screamed and Grave Eagle, excited by the sound, yelled the war whoop of the Sioux as he struck with the side of the tomahawk. Johnson fell, stunned, a thin trickle of blood running from beneath his white hair. Grave Eagle screamed his challenge again, the terrible war whoop designed to paralyse enemies with fear so that they would fall easy victims, then quickly gathered up the halters, sprang on to the big gelding and, drumming his heels against the animal's flanks, rode into the night.

'The horses!' Lamont, standing by the whiskey wagon heard the drumming of hooves. 'Someone's stealing the horses!'

Mike, standing on top of the wagon,

had a better view. The night was dark but the fires and lanterns of the camp cast a dull glow for some distance around. In that glow he could see vague shapes and, instinctively, raised his Colt and thumbed the hammer.

Grave Eagle was an impossible target. He lay crouched over the gelding, his body blending with that of the horse. He used an old Indian trick, throwing himself to one side so that only his head showed from beneath the neck of the horse. He grunted as lead whined above him, knowing that he was perfectly safe.

Mike knew it too. He lowered the Colt and jumped down from the wagon.

'Get horses,' he ordered. 'Saddle up and we'll get after him.' He led the way to the corral. 'How's the old man?'

'Dead.' A brawny railroad worker stooped over the limp figure. 'I reckon his skull's bashed in.'

'You sure?' Mike stooped and thrust his hand beneath Johnson's shirt. 'He's not dead, only stunned. Bring water and some of that whiskey.'

The whiskey pedlar, forgotten in the excitement, came forward with a pannikin of his special brew. It was good stuff meant for his own consumption. Mike took it, tasted it, waited until a bucket of water had brought the old man to some awareness, then tipped the burning spirit into his mouth.

Johnson coughed, spluttered, then stared at the ring of faces.

'Did you get him?'

'Who?' Mike gave the old man more whiskey. 'Take it easy and don't hurry. Was it an Indian?'

'Yes, a Sioux from the way he wore his hair.' Johnson shuddered and felt at his head. 'I thought he was going to scalp me for sure.'

'Was he wearing paint?'

'No,' admitted the old man. He rubbed the lump on his head. 'First time I knew an Indian not take a scalp when he had the chance.'

'We stopped him,' said Lamont. He

shouted towards some men saddling horses. 'Hurry! Get those horses fixed and get after him.'

'You won't catch him,' said Mike. 'You'll never trail him in the dark.'

'We were attacked,' said Lamont. 'That sneaking redskin came here to steal our horses and would have collected Johnson's scalp, if we hadn't acted so fast.'

'We weren't attacked,' corrected Mike. He looked at Johnson. 'How many Indians did you see?'

'Just the one.'

'Was he wearing feathers?'

'Not that I remember.' The old man rubbed his head again. 'I only had time for one look but he didn't seem very big to me. Didn't come much higher than my shoulder.'

'A young warrior out to collect coup,' said Mike. He looked at Lamont. 'This was no Indian raid, just a simple case of horse stealing. Had that Indian been on the warpath he would have collected Johnson's scalp before getting the horses. No need to get all excited about it.'

'No?' Lamont ground his teeth in anger. 'That damn Indian has stolen my favourite gelding. He's taken two other horses, too, both of prime stock. I want them back.'

'You won't get them by chasing after him in the dark,' said Mike. 'Wait until the pow-wow and then ask Red Arrow to return them. If he wants peace, and I think he does, he'll send them back.'

'That's not good enough,' snapped Lamont. 'That redskin stole my horses and he's got to be punished.' He turned to the watchful men. 'That right, men? We've got to teach these red devils to leave white men's property alone.'

They nodded, in full agreement, and Mike could guess how they felt. In the West a man's horse was his treasured possession for, quite literally, it meant life itself. A horse thief did more than rob a man of a valuable animal, he endangered the owner's life itself for a horse was often the sole means of transportation. Horse thieves were lynched without question. They were hung up to the nearest tree and left as a grim warning to others. It was a rough, quick justice dictated by necessity.

'Take it easy,' said Mike. 'So the Indian stole some horses, so what? You'll get them back.'

'Maybe.' Lamont took his pistol from its holster, checked the loading, thrust it back into leather. He grabbed at a saddled horse and, mounting, stared down at the men.

'Listen,' he yelled. 'We were minding our own business and harming no one when this lousy redskin came in and attacked us. He tried to kill Johnson and would have done had we not scared him off. He was after scalps and horses. Johnson's lucky to still be alive and so are a lot more of us. If he hadn't given the warning that Indian would have lifted hair all through the night. As it is he almost killed the old man and has ridden off with our horses. Is it good enough?'

'No!' A big man, his thick arms covered with tattoo marks, shook his fist towards the hills. 'Those damn Indians should be wiped out.'

'That's right!' Another man joined in. He was followed by a third, a fourth, until it seemed that most of the camp was yelling for Indian blood.

It was natural, for long months now they had worked and lived with the fear of an Indian attack and Grave Eagle had merely served as an excuse. Lamont, quick to take advantage of circumstances, saw the perfect way to trigger off an Indian war and so gain his own ends.

Mike saw it too.

'Hold it!' He mounted a horse, holding the animal as it moved restlessly beneath him. 'There's a big peace talk coming off tomorrow at the new fort. You'll get your horses back and there'll be no danger of attacks of any kind. There wasn't one tonight. All that happened was that a young warrior wanted to find out how good he was. If

208

you go off half-cocked now you'll start something you won't be able to finish.'

'Indian Lover!' yelled a man. 'We don't want none of that talk.'

'That's right.' Lamont stared at the men. 'There's only one thing these Indians understand and that's force. They raided us and stole our horses. All right, they can't grumble if we return the compliment.' He rose in his stirrups and pointed towards the dark hills. 'There's an Indian village out there. What say we do with it?'

'Burn it,' yelled a man.

'Wipe it out,' shrieked another.

'Stamp the red swine into the dirt!'

'Are you crazy!' Mike felt for his guns then halted the gesture as he saw Lamont's expression. If he tried force the big man would kill him. Mike knew it and so tried persuasion instead. 'If you ride against that village you'll be wiped out. It's dark and you're all half-drunk anyway. Those Indians have scouts out and they'll give warning. I tell you that you haven't got a chance.'

'Indian Lover,' yelled the man again. He waved his arms. 'What are we waiting for?'

'Where's the whiskey?' A huge negro made the suggestion and the others took it up with a roar. Within seconds the barrels of rot-gut had been pulled from the wagon, their snake-contents forgotten, and pannikins were passed from hand to hand as the heads were broached and the spirit distributed. Mike edged his horse towards Lamont. 'You know what you're doing?'

'I think so.'

'You're setting these men against the Indians. You know that?'

'Well?'

'If these men ride against that village tonight it will mean an Indian war. The pow-wow will be called off and the chance of a lasting peace thrown away. Is that what you want?'

Lamont smiled.

'I guess you do,' said Mike. 'And we both know why.' He stared towards the men clustered around the wagon. 'Ride against the Indians and those men will lose their hair for sure. Is that what you want?'

'I don't think that you are an Indian Lover,' said Lamont. 'I wouldn't call you that, but you seem to forget that you're a white man. The Sioux raided this camp tonight, they stole horses and almost killed a man. You know that, you saw it.'

'One young warrior getting himself some fun,' said Mike disgustedly. 'Call that a raid?'

'Yes, and so will other white men.' Lamont stared at Mike. 'Keep out of this, Wilson. These men have had enough of Indians and they know what they're doing. So what if the peace talks fail? Am I supposed to worry about that? I don't care if every last Indian is made a good dead Indian. The railroad must go through.'

'That isn't your reason.' Mike shifted in his saddle. The scene around the whiskey wagon had grown wilder as the men gulped the raw brew. The pedlar, after one wild protest, had been shoved head-first in an empty barrel and after freeing himself, had decided to let things take their course. Mike hoped that the men would drink themselves incapable.

Lamont had also seen that danger. He rode forward and fired a shot into the air.

'Get your guns,' he shouted. 'Get your horses. Ride double if you have to but let's get going.' He fired again, the sharp sound echoing over the prairie. 'Come on, men. let's have ourselves some fun.'

'We're having fun.' said the big negro. 'Lots of it.'

'You're getting drunk,' said Lamont. 'You know what will happen soon? The Indians will be riding down on us ready to lift hair. You'll be too drunk to stop them and they'll do as they like with you. Torture you, perhaps, tie you to a pair of horses and pull out your arms and legs. Is that what you want?'

Lamont was shrewd, he knew how to

play on their fears.

'Johnson's had his head bashed in,' he yelled. 'An old man like that got himself tomahawked by a stinking Indian. You going to let them get away with that?'

'No,' yelled the negro. He dipped his pannikin into the whiskey barrel, took a final drink and flung the container to one side.

'No!' Mike tried to stop them. 'Don't do it!'

He was swept aside as men rushed towards the waiting horses. They were armed each with a six-gun and cartridge belt. Some had rifles and all carried knives. A few were relatively steady on their feet but the majority swayed and had to be helped into the saddle. Almost a hundred men, many riding double, assembled behind Lamont.

He stared at them, smiling as he saw the hate in their eyes, the eagerness to get to grips with the Indians they hated. He rode forward and snatched up some brands from one of the fires and passed them around.

'We'll need fire to burn their tepees,' he said. 'Ready! Let's go!'

They moved after the big railroad boss, a yelling, swaying, semi-drunken mob. They were like a gang of schoolboys out on a spree, none of them, aside from Lamont, knowing what they were heading into. Later, as the night air turned the whiskey fumes in their heads, they would turn mean and cruel. They would want to burn and kill and destroy with a savage fury against the Indians.

Mike watched them go. He knew that only luck would permit any of them to see the dawn. They were riding against experts in the art of open warfare, a shouting, fire-carrying mob doomed to almost certain destruction. But before they died they would set the prairie ablaze.

Turning his mount the tall man dug in his spurs and rode into the night.

11

The fort was so new that it had no official name but was called Fort Clarke out of respect to the man who had built it. It rested on a rolling bank close to a winding river and was flanked by the wooded slopes of gentle hills. The thick logs from which it was constructed still oozed sap and resinous gums so that the air was heavy with the scent of new-cut timber and pine.

It was a small fort, a high stockade, a watch-tower, a couple of wide doors and the usual interior buildings. From it the garrison could control the heart of the Indian Nations and the slow but steady progress of the railroad which was winding like a shining snake over land which had previously only known the tread of the red man, the hooves of horse and buffalo, or the occasional passage of some lone prospector or surveyor.

Towards it, just as the rising sun had cast a pearl-grey light in the east, a solitary horseman made his way.

A sentry in the watch-tower saw him and gave the word. A sergeant joined the sentry and stared through binoculars at the lone rider.

'White man,' he said. 'His horse is about to drop. Better send out to him.'

Three men accompanied the sergeant as he rode towards the distant figure. Before they had covered more than half the gap between them the horse stumbled, fell, lay still. The rider, thrown from the animal, staggered to his feet and, after examining his mount, began to walk towards the still-distant fort.

'Wilson!' The sergeant reined in beside the tall man. 'I thought you was at the rail-camp with Lamont.'

Mike rubbed his hand over his burning eyes.

'I was.' Mike rubbed his hand over

his burning eyes. 'Get me to the general.'

'Sure. Can you get up behind me?'

'I'll try.' Mike tried and failed. He was too stiff with long riding to do more than make the attempt. 'Sorry. I guess that I can't make it.'

'We'll help.' The sergeant gestured to his men and a pair of strong arms lifted the tall man to the back of the horse. 'Hold on.'

'I'm holding.' Mike swore when he saw what the sergeant was doing. 'Not that way, man! To the fort.'

'Don't you want your saddle and other gear?' The sergeant twisted his head so as to look at Mike. 'And what about the horse?'

'Dead.'

'Sure? I wouldn't want it to suffer.'

'It's done all the suffering it's going to,' said Mike. 'It broke his heart trying to do the impossible. And I dumped the saddle a long time ago.' He grunted as the jolting of the horse reminded him of his stiffness. 'I had to lighten the animal,' he explained. 'I've come from the rail-camp in one night. Couldn't expect the beast to carry a load of leather as well as a man.'

'Trouble?' The sergeant had served a long time on the frontier and he knew that a man who threw away his saddle and killed his horse must be carrying bad news.

'Get me to the general,' said Mike. 'Fast.'

'Hang on,' said the sergeant and dug in his spurs.

General Clarke was up and dressed in his best uniform by the time Mike arrived. Today was the day of the great pow-wow with Red Arrow and, knowing the Indians' love of ceremony on important occasions, the General had dressed the part. His uniform was pressed and spotless, his boots and belts, pistol holder and the scabbard of the long sabre were polished until they shone. As he was so were the officers and men of the tiny garrison. The compound had been swept clean and everything was ready as for inspection.

Now he awaited the arrival of the Indians.

'A fine day. Captain.' he said to the officer at his side. 'This will be the first time you've dealt with the Indians, isn't it?'

'Yes, sir.' Captain Fromach was a very young graduate of West Point with high ideas as to his own capabilities. Clarke entered.

'Then you're due for an interesting experience,' said the general. 'The Indians are a proud people and must be treated as such. No laughter, jokes or smiles at anything they may say or do. Never display impatience or any emotion. Never regard them as savages or as inferiors.'

'No, sir.'

'Remember that,' said the General. He turned as the sergeant came up to him, saluted, whispered in his ear.

'Wilson?' Clarke looked startled. 'Here?'

'Yes, sir. I've just brought him in.

219

He's in a bad way. His partner is with him now.'

'I'll be right down.' Clarke bit his lips as he glanced over the parapet. The peace talks were due to start at dawn, or rather when the sun had risen above the trees at the crest of the hill. Then the day would still be cool and the talks, usually long and involved, could be held in comfort.

'Let me know as soon as Red Arrow shows up,' he ordered. Fromach saluted as the general ran down the stairs towards his office.

Mike was waiting for him. He sat, legs outstretched, a cigar smouldering between his lips. He removed it as Clark entered.

'Mind if I don't stand up, General? I'm all in and would like to rest for a while.'

'The sergeant tells me you rode in from the rail-camp,' said Clarke. 'That's a long way to come in a single night.'

'It is.'

'Trouble?'

'Bad trouble.' Mike put down the cigar. 'Lamont's gone on the warpath. A young warrior of the Sioux stole some horses last night and knocked out the guard. He could have killed him but didn't, just put him to sleep. The Indian got away with three horses.'

'So?'

'So Lamont got his men and went out to raid the Indian village. There was a whiskey pedlar in camp and the men had a skinful before they started.'

'I see.' Clarke took three long strides down the length of the room, turned, strode back to Mike. 'Did you try to stop them?'

'Did everything but shoot them down. Lamont was set on burning the village. I told him that he would start a war if he did it, but it didn't worry him. I think that he wants to start a war anyway.' He told the general of his suspicions as to the gold strike. 'So you can see how it is. Red Arrow won't stand for his village being attacked and will go to war over it.'

'He is due for the parley this morning,' said the General. 'Hell! We could have fixed up a new treaty without trouble.' He looked at Mike. 'Maybe we still can.'

'Maybe.' The tall man wasn't hopeful. 'But will you be allowed to? For my money those railroad men got themselves killed last night. If the Indians didn't fight then they wiped out the village. No Indian will let white men do that to their tepees. My guess is that Lamont knew what would happen. He probably ducked out as soon as the fighting started and he knew which way things were going. Now that the Indians have killed some men the cavalry will have to move in to protect the railroad. That means the Indians will hit back and there's your Indian war.'

'I see.' Clarke looked at the tall man. 'So you rode here at top speed. Why?'

'This fort is right in the heart of the Nations. If the word spreads and the Sioux go on the warpath then it will be attacked. You were expecting a pow-wow, you might get something you didn't bargain for. I rode to give you warning.'

'You rode faster than any man I know,' said the General, slowly. 'Red Arrow must be around here somewhere, Mike, so he couldn't have heard what happened last night. With any sort of luck at all we can still make the treaty.'

'And after?'

'If we sign a treaty with the Indians it will wash out all that has gone before. If Red Arrow doesn't know of Lamont's attack then we needn't tell him. He won't know that we know so we will have something up our sleeve. He can't know and there's no reason for him not to sign. The trick is for us to get him to sign before word reaches him about the attack.'

General Clarke strode down the room again. He was nervous, knowing how little chance his garrison would have if attacked by Indians and yet ready to take the risk in order to prevent an uprising.

'You better stay out of sight, Wilson. We don't want you seen by an Indian who knows you were at the railcamp.'

'May I make a suggestion?'

'Certainly.'

'We don't know what will happen. Red Arrow may sign the treaty or he may not. He may keep it after he learns what has happened at the village or he may not. One thing is for sure, if there's an uprising the Nations will be swarming with Indians on the warpath. How about sending back to Fort Hemridge for more men?'

'I've thought of that.' The General nodded at the tall man. 'But it will take time for a message to reach them and longer for them to get here. It may not be necessary to send for them at all.'

'They can't do any harm even if they only come for the ride,' said Mike. 'Send right away and order them to get here. If the fort is attacked then they can save it by attacking the Indians from the rear. If the peace lasts then they can give a demonstration of the strength of the cavalry. In any case if war does start this is where they should be. From this fort they can hold the heart of the Nations.'

'You're right,' said the General. 'I'll send right away.' He frowned. 'The trouble is that I've so few men here at this time. If I send a uniformed man to Fort Hemridge the Indians may get suspicious. Red Arrow is a crafty old man and he'll wonder why I am sending for fresh troops if I intend to make and keep a new treaty. I can't afford to have him think like that.'

'Then send a civilian.' Mike pointed towards Sam. 'I can't go, I'm too saddle sore and worn, but Sam can. Give him a message, a good horse and some food and he'll make Fort Hemridge in good time. Right, Sam?'

'Sure.'

'All right.' Clarke opened the door of the room and called outside. 'Sergeant!'

'Yes, sir!'

'I'll write a message,' said the

General as the soldier saluted and left. 'You can give it to Commander Denton. 'You know what it will say.'

'I know.' Sam looked at Mike. 'Will you be joining me at the fort?'

'No.' Mike stretched. 'I'll stay here.' He smiled at the young man. 'Don't worry about me, Sam, and don't worry about the Indians. Just get on that horse and ride as fast as you can.' He smiled again as the young man nodded and left. Sam, despite his youth, was turning out to be a regular frontiersman.

Alone, Mike rested for a while, dozing in the chair, reliving again the events of the wild ride when he had literally ridden a horse to death to bring the warning to the fort. A cook brought him hot coffee laced with brandy and he gulped it, feeling some of the tiredness leave his body. The cook returned for the empty cup and Mike questioned him.

'Pow-wow started yet?'

'Been on for an hour,' said the cook.

'Red Arrow and about twenty or more warriors all dressed in robes and feathers and smoking the peace pipe with the General and the Captain. You going to take a look?'

'Why not?'

Mike rose and stretched himself. Long habit made him check the loading of the twin Colts which hung at his waist and, lighting a cigar, he left the room and went outside. Caution prevented him from exposing himself so he climbed the watch-tower and stood beside the guard. The roofed enclosure set high above the compound afforded a wide view of the country and the scene below but prevented a clear view of the occupants.

'Pretty, ain't it?' The guard nodded to where a table had been set just outside the open doors of the fort. General Clarke and Captain Fromach sat at the table while, to each side and behind them, the garrison stood with grounded rifles. Before the table, squatting on the ground, Red Arrow, Lame Horse, Bent

Feather and some other warriors gravely listened and argued at the terms of the proposed peace treaty.

It was a lengthy business this arguing. Clarke could not give the Indians the reassurance they wanted. He could not promise that the fort would be destroyed and the railroad abolished. Instead he spoke of the benefits cheap transportation would bring to the Indians and tried hard to get Red Arrow to make a promise that there would be no war between the two races.

Red Arrow, in turn, refused to compromise. He had justice on his side, the white men had broken their word, and he insisted on the impossible. Clarke knew that it was impossible, even if he made the required promises they would be broken immediately. All he could hope to do was to gain time and prevent an immediate war.

Again and again he urged Red Arrow to sign a fresh agreement. He promised that he would confer with high officials back east, try and set aside new lands for the Indians, swore that, from this time on, no violence would be offered the villages. He was not so much after a lasting treaty as one which would safeguard the country from the effects of Lamont's recklessness. Once Red Arrow signed an agreement the Indian Chief would keep to his word for the term of his promise. General Clarke could only hope that some means of settling the Indian problem would have been found before it expired.

'Getting warm,' said the sentry in the watch-tower. 'Going to be a hot afternoon.'

'Let me have your glasses.' Mike took the binoculars and held them to his eyes. Far across the rolling hills, lifting like a thin thread of darkness against the clear blue of the sky, something climbed towards the brassy heavens. Even as Mike watched the thin thread broke, resolved itself into a series of puffs, then rose steadily again.

'What is it?' The guard was curious.

'Smoke signal.' Mike swung down the

glasses and searched the hills near at hand. From among the trees at the crest of the hill a thin plume of smoke rose slowly skywards. 'Get down to the meeting and tell the General to get back inside the fort.' Mike stared at the sentry. 'Move!'

'I can't do that.' The soldier shook his head. 'I'd get jailed if I deserted my post. And what would the General say if I busted up his meeting?'

'He'll be dead if you don't,' said Mike grimly. 'That smoke means trouble.' He lifted the glasses again and far in the distance saw a mounted Indian riding hard towards the fort. Behind the Indian galloped a second horse, something heavy and shapeless bouncing on its back.

'Sound the alarm,' he snapped out to the sentry. 'Quick!'

The man hesitated, then, lifting his bugle, he sounded the alarm. As the clear notes echoed over the fort the General turned, staring up at the watch tower. Mike leaned out, made a sweeping gesture with his palm, then held out his hand, thumb down.

Clarke caught the gesture, realized what it meant, and tried to save something from the wreckage. Red Arrow had come under a flag of truce and had been promised safe conduct. If he ever hoped to be trusted by the Indians again the General knew that he had to honour that safe conduct. He turned to Captain Fromach.

'Get the men inside the fort. Quick!'

'What is it, sir?'

'Trouble.'

'Indian trouble?'

'Yes, you young fool. Now do as I say.' The General was impatient. He wanted to call off the parley and get inside the fort before the Indians knew anything was wrong. The alternative was to break his given word to Red Arrow or run the risk of having his men attacked outside cover. Red Arrow would honour his word, yes, but it would take but a single shot to convert the peaceful scene into a shambles.

And the General knew that Red Arrow's warriors were thick in the woods around the fort.

He rose to his feet, nodded to the Indian Chief, and watched as his men sloped arms and filed back into the fort. Red Arrow watched them, his face expressionless; then, as he glanced towards the horizon, his face hardened.

'It is war,' he said. 'The white men have attacked our village.' He spoke in rapid Sioux to his warriors, then faced the general. 'The smoke tells of war. You spoke with a forked tongue when you spoke of peace.'

'I know nothing of what happened,' said the General. 'You say there is war but it is not of my choosing.'

'I think that you speak true,' said Red Arrow. He stood, tall and proud. 'Hear my words. We came to pow-wow and have smoked the pipe of peace. I shall not break that peace. But between us there is war for the smoke does not lie. We shall leave you now and go in peace. We will return as enemies. I have spoken.'

He turned and, followed by his men, began to walk away. Captain Fromach stared at the departing warriors in disgust, then, snatching his pistol from his belt, he pointed it at Red Arrow.

'Stand where you are!'

Red Arrow did not halt.

'Stop, you red devil, or I'll kill you!'

The Chief halted and stared at the captain.

'You're a prisoner. You're all prisoners!' Fromach smiled at the General. 'This is the way to handle these savages. Once they know we've got their chief they'll soon come to heel.' His gloved hand tightened on the pistol. It was cocked and needed only a touch on the hair trigger to send lead smashing into the Indians. Clarke stepped forward.

'Put that gun away, you fool. Put it away!'

'Not until we have taken them prisoner, sir.' Fromach gestured with the pistol. 'All you swine. Walk into the fort with your hands held above

233

your head. Move!'

Red Arrow looked at the captain. He looked at the general, tight lipped but unable to do anything until the captain had put away the gun. When he did so, the general promised himself, he would be court-martialled for insubordination. But that was no help now and a scuffle between officers before the Indians and the garrison was unthinkable.

Red Arrow stared at the two officers for a long time, then, deliberately, began to walk away.

Captain Fromach fired.

He was normally a good shot but the general had acted as his finger closed on the trigger. The bullet did not hit the target for which it was meant. Red Arrow was unharmed but his brother, Lame Horse the Shaman, groaned and sank to his knees, blood pouring from his mouth.

Red Arrow stared at the dying man, screamed with a terrible rage and, his arm moving so fast that it was a blur, drew the long knife at his belt. It flashed in the sun as it lanced towards the captain's throat. It struck and blood spilled over the immaculate uniform. Then the Indians were running, carrying the body of Lame Horse, and the general, staggering beneath his burden, carried Fromach to the fort. Above him, from the firing step, the sound of rifles cut the air as the soldiers fired after the vanishing Indians.

Above the sound of the firing came another sound; deep, ominous, rolling like muted thunder over the Indian Nations.

The war drums of the Sioux.

12

Red Arrow stood in a clearing in the woods and stared at the white man held by two warriors before him. Lamont seemed to have shrivelled, his bigness somehow vanishing in his fear. He sweated continually, his shirt was dark with perspiration, his face blanched as he stared at the Chief.

'Dog!' Red Arrow stared his contempt. 'You led your warriors against the lodges of the Sioux and many were slain. Did you think to take Indians with such fools?'

'It was a mistake,' babbled Lamont. 'They got drunk and were wild at the loss of the horses. I tried to stop them.'

'You led them,' said the Chief impassively. 'Grave Eagle knows the white man's tongue. You tried to burn and kill the old men and the squaws.' He did not smile, war was too serious for smiles, but a proud light glittered in the eyes of Red Arrow. 'My warriors took many scalps from those men who rode against us. Many guns, many horses. The white squaws have much cause to wail.'

'You won,' said Lamont sickly. 'You massacred my men. Isn't that enough?'

'He who was my brother has gone from among us,' said Red Arrow. Like all Indians he did not mention the dead by name. To do so would have called back their spirits and brought bad luck. 'He has gone — but you remain.'

'Let me go,' said Lamont. 'What are you going to do with me?'

'A brave man does not whine at the thought of death.' Red Arrow made a gesture. 'Be brave, white man, and die like an Indian.'

'No!' Lamont trembled in his fear. 'Don't kill me. Don't kill me.' He tore himself away from the warriors and threw himself to the ground before Red Arrow. 'I'll give you money, lots of money. I'll tell you a secret. You could be rich. Rich, understand! You could have lots of gold, yellow iron, to trade for guns and blankets and beads. Lots of yellow iron. It's in the hills. I know where it is and can show you. Only let me live. Please let me live!'

Red Arrow made a sign.

'No!' Lamont twisted with desperate frenzy. He had heard of the tortures Indians inflicted on their prisoners. Some were buried to the neck and molasses poured over their heads to attract the ants. When the syrup was eaten the insects tore the living flesh from the skull beneath. Or a prisoner would be staked out on the ground and a rattle-snake, tethered by a rawhide thong, would be set near him. The thong was just too short to permit the snake bite but, as evening fell and the dampness moistened the rawhide, it stretched allowing the snake more freedom. The long, dragging hours of waiting were sheer mental agony.

There were other tortures, a thong around the head tightened with a stick so that the eyes bulged from their sockets, flaming splinters beneath the fingernails, flaying and burning. Lamont, in imagination, died a thousand deaths.

The warriors seized him, dragged him towards a waiting horse, bound his hands behind his back and threw him to the ground. A warrior mounted the horse, a length of rope held in his hand. The other end was made into a noose and passed over Lamont's feet. It was tightened and the mounted warrior, with a wild yell, bounded forward dragging the helpless man behind him.

He wove skilfully through trees, emerged on the small plain in which stood the fort, and galloped towards it. After him, bobbing and bouncing like a ball, his face streaming blood where the skin had been stripped from the bone, his mouth clogged with leaves and his body a mass of bruises, tumbled Lamont.

Mike, standing on the firing step, his Winchester in his hands, stared at the lone rider and his peculiar burden.

'Hell, that's a man he's dragging behind him.' A soldier, his face white, threw up his rifle and took a shot at the Indian. He missed, the warrior had thrown himself sidewise so that only a slim brown leg and a painted face were visible. He yelled his derision as the soldier missed and fired back in return.

Mike waited, knowing the range was too great for accurate shooting and then, as the pony began to circle away from the fort, he squeezed the trigger of his rifle.

He didn't aim for the warrior, the target was too small, instead he fired at the pony and sent lead crashing into its heart. The pony fell, the Indian rolling head over heels as he hit the ground. Mike fired again, a second time, then with one bound he was over the parapet, was hanging by one hand and then let himself drop to the ground twenty feet below.

Before the soldiers had guessed what he was doing he was running towards

240

the dead pony, the bound man and the shot Indian.

He stooped over the red-stained mass, glanced at the Indian, then ran back towards the fort. Behind him, from the shelter of the trees, the screaming war whoop of the Sioux echoed across the plain and a cloud of warriors, stooped over their mounts, came bursting towards the fort.

'Open the gate,' ordered the general. 'Quick!'

The massive doors opened then slammed shut as Mike darted through. Immediately a ragged burst of firing came from the soldiers as they fired at the screaming Indians. In return bullets and arrows began to hum towards the fort, some hitting the thick logs, some aimed too high but others finding a resting place in living flesh.

'It was Lamont,' said Mike, briefly. 'Dead.' He glanced at the General. 'And the Captain?'

'Died a few minutes ago.' Clarke frowned. 'The stupid, young fool! Still, he paid for his idiocy with his life.'

'Lamont's paid too,' said Mike grimly. 'The pity is that he only had one life to give.' He ducked as an arrow came lancing towards him, shot high so that it would fall into the compound. 'I sure hope that Sam made it.'

'If he didn't we're in trouble,' said Clarke. 'We've few men, little water and not too much ammunition. The fort was only finished a few days ago and supplies were due this week.' He bit his lips. 'It isn't going to be easy.'

'We'll make out,' said Mike. He glanced up as another arrow dug into the ground at his feet. 'Better get some water buckets ready. They'll be trying fire-arrows soon.'

'I hope not. We haven't the water to spare.'

'Get some blankets then, wet them, and have men beat out the arrows as they land.' A bullet whined from a post with a shrill hum and a man screamed as the ricochetting ball struck him in the back. He spun, his rifle falling from his nerveless hands, and the sound of his impact as he hit the ground was horrible to hear.

'I'd better get up there,' said Mike. 'Things seem to be warming up.'

They were.

The Indians had broken from their original charge and were now circling the fort. They rode fast, crouched over their ponies, firing or shooting their arrows as they rode. The arrows were the barbed shafts used for war and, impelled from the powerful bows of buffalo horn, could kill as surely as a rifle. In some respects they were more deadly than a rifle for the arrows could be slanted in the air to fall within the compound or sent across the fort to land on the opposite firing platform.

Mike walked the firing platform giving short words of advice to the soldiers. He walked and spoke with an air of command and the men, recognizing it, listened to him and obeyed him.

'Watch your shots,' he ordered. 'We're low on ammunition so make every bullet count. Wait until you get a good sight of an Indian. Follow your target and squeeze the trigger. Keep calm, you've more chance of getting them than they have of getting you.'

The last was simple truth. It is always easier for a stationary man to hit a moving object than for a moving man to hit a stationary one. Several feathered bodies and dead ponies outside the fort gave mute testimony to that fact.

But the defenders had lost men too.

They lay where they had fallen, some with the red-rimmed holes of bullets, others with the feathered shafts of arrows buried in their flesh. There were more Indians than soldiers, many more, and every soldier who died weakened the line of defence.

High above the sun crawled across the sky and sank flaming into the west. The Indians had drawn away from the fort taking their dead and wounded with them, and the hungry soldiers were enjoying a meal of beans, bacon corn bread and coffee. General Clarke walked the firing platform and examined the structure. The thick logs were chipped and scarred but had easily withstood the fire. Mike, walking with him, touched the surface of the logs, and rubbed the stickiness from his fingers.

'The heat's drawing the resin from the timbers,' he said. 'Couldn't you use other than pine?'

'Not and get the fort built in the time.' Clarke stared into the mounting darkness. 'Think they'll make a night attack?'

'Might, be unusual if they do.' The tall man stared upwards. 'No moon tonight though it's clear and the stars should give us light.' He led the way down from the platform. 'How's the ammunition holding out?'

'It's not.' The General kicked some spent cases from underfoot. 'We'll have to hold our fire until it will do the most good. That means the Indians can ride closer to the fort and take better aim.'

'The wounded?'

'The surgeon's working on them. The walking wounded are detailed as fire-guards.'

'Fair enough.' Mike yawned. 'I think I'll get some rest. Better put a couple of men in the watch-tower, General. One man can't look two ways at once.'

Leaving the general, Mike entered the dormitory and sank down on a vacant bunk. He unbuckled his gunbelt and hung it on a peg and then, without even removing his boots, fell into a light, dream-haunted sleep.

He awoke to the screams of men and the smell of burning.

Fire lapped against one of the interior buildings and, as he staggered from the bunk-house buckling on his guns, a wave of thick smoke blinded him and filled his lungs. Coughing he staggered clear and saw bandaged men beating with wet blankets at blazing timbers.

'Douse it!' Mike jumped forward and snatched a bucket. 'You'll never beat it

246

out. Wash it down.' Tipping the bucket he flung the contents over the burning timbers and reached for another. It took six buckets before the blaze was under control and not until the leaping fire had died to smouldering embers did the tall man climb down to the firing platform.

'Fire arrows?'

'Yes.' General Clarke nursed a roughly bandaged arm. 'They must have crawled to within a few feet of the stockade. First thing we knew was a volley fired at the watchtower, both sentries dead. They followed it with a shower of arrows, some with fire, some without. We lost ten men and they started three fires. You put out the last one.'

'Red Arrow knows his business,' said Mike grimly. 'He knows just how many men are in this garrison, you paraded them for his inspection. He knows that they can't stay awake all the time and that we must be short of water. He's going to keep attacking to make us jump. After a while he'll attack in full force and we'll be overrun.' He glanced at the sky. 'Dawn's only an hour off. Why did you let me sleep so long?'

'You needed the rest and the night was quiet.'

'It's woken up then.' Mike watched the flaming path of a fire-arrow. It soared high into the air and then plummetted into the compound. Another followed it, a third, and then a whole shower of them. Men swore as they stamped and beat out the grease-soaked rags with which the shafts were bound. Some of the soldiers began firing into the darkness.

'Stop them!' said Mike. 'They're only wasting cartridges.'

The general nodded and yelled orders to cease fire. He sighed as he leaned against the parapet.

'Think Sam can make it?'

'Hard to tell.' Mike watched as the night slowly grew lighter with the oyster-greyness of the false dawn. 'I'd say yes. But he's got a long way to travel and then the troops have got to get back here. Even with fools' luck they can't be here for several days. We'll just have to sweat it out until they come.'

'Or until Red Arrow overruns the fort,' said Clarke sombrely.

Mike shrugged.

The day grew bright and the sun burned down from the heavens. Again the Indians charged around the fort, shooting, firing their flaming arrows, causing the few defenders to waste their precious water to kill the flames. Night came and with it the threat of fire. Again day, again night in a mounting procession of terrible strain and constant warfare with the sharp explosions of the rifles mingling with the hum of arrows and the war whoops of the Indians.

'We're beaten,' said the General on the morning of the seventh day. 'The water's all gone and the ammunition's low. We've lost too many men and the few that are left can hardly stand for tiredness.' His face sagged with his defeat. 'It looks like the end.'

'Remember Lamont?' Mike rubbed the stubble on his chin and finished checking his Colts. 'Remember how they treated him?'

'Don't remind me.'

'That's how they'll kill us if they capture us alive,' said Mike. 'You know that, don't you?'

'I know it.'

'Then let's have no more talk of defeat.' The tall man spun the chambers of his weapons and thrust them into their holsters. 'We'll fight until the last man is dead. We'll fight while we have a bullet between us and when they're gone, we'll use clubbed rifles, sabres, anything. Tell the men the worst thing that can happen to them is to be taken alive. Tell them to remember Lamont.'

'I'll tell them,' said the general. 'But men can only do so much.' He walked away, staggering slightly from weakness and tiredness. Mike watched him, then looked out over the plain. Around the fort, just as they had ridden for the past seven days, the warriors of the Sioux swirled in a constant mass.

The destruction of the fort was important to Red Arrow. Once gone the heart of the Indian Nations would be freed of the white man and he could send his warriors to harry and burn far to the east. As it was he had destroyed the furthermost rail-camps, had scalped and killed isolated groups of settlers, and had made the trails impassable for any but a heavily armed body of men.

But the new fort remained a thorn in his side. He hated it for what it represented and for the threat to his safety. He had sworn to destroy it.

He rode towards the structure as the sun mounted towards the zenith, Bent Feather at his side. News had come from hard-riding scouts and the Great Chief was worried.

'So word reached the Long Knives,' he said. 'How did this thing happen?'

'No soldier has ridden between the forts,' said Bent Feather. 'One white man left before the pow-wow. We saw him but did not stop him. We were at peace.'

'Now we are at war.' Red Arrow glanced up at the sun. 'Have warriors lie in wait so that they may shoot at the Long Knives when they ride past. Tell all warriors that the fort must be taken before another dawn or we must leave it standing.'

'We can meet the Long Knives,' said Bent Feather. 'Let us face them and kill.'

'That is not the way we must fight this war.' Red Arrow stared into the distance. 'Our strength is not the strengh of the white man. Once he meets us he will crush us for our warriors are unskilled in the way of the white man's war. We must ride fast and destroy quick. Kill and ride away, strike as the snake strikes and fight like the swoop of the eagle.'

'Can we win such a war?'

'We can win no other.' Red Arrow rode down towards the fort to lead his men into battle.

Mike saw him come, recognized the head-dress for what it was and, snatching up his rifle, took careful aim. He trembled a little as he took his sight and cursed the weakness which blurred his vision. Little sleep, little water, scant food and the constant exertion of fighting back the Indians and putting out the fires they had started with their fire-arrows had reduced the garrison to a bleary-eyed, hollow-cheeked travesty of themselves.

The Winchester seemed very heavy, the shock of the recoil almost more than he had expected. Mike levered another precious cartridge into the breech and swore as he saw Red Arrow, still mounted on his pony, riding towards the fort.

Again the tall man took careful aim but, even as his finger closed on the trigger, a warrior bounded before the Chief. The bullet caught him high in the body, threw him to one side, and left him kicking on the ground. Before Mike could reload Red Arrow had passed around the angle of the stockade and a shower of bullets and arrows forced the tall man to take cover.

'Get him?' The general had watched with interest knowing that only a good reason would have made Mike use ammunition.

'No.'

'A pity.' Clarke tried to moisten his lips with a cracked and swollen tongue. He lifted himself and stared towards the river, so near and yet so unreachable. 'I think that, given the chance, I could drink that stream dry.'

'Don't think about it,' said Mike. 'Suck a bullet, a stone, anything, but get your mind off that river.'

'How can I?' The General stared down into the fort. Of his original command only ten men were left unwounded and another ten who could hold and fire a rifle. Of the rest most were dead and the others were so badly hurt as to be helpless. Their cries and moans as they begged for water echoed from the dormitories.

'Poor devils,' said the general. 'They're burning for water and we can't give them any. There isn't a drop within the fort. If Red Arrow rushed us now I doubt if we could beat him off.'

'We would,' said Mike grimly. 'We'd have to.' He looked up as the sentry in the watch-tower yelled the alarm. 'Quick! To your posts!'

Slowly the men dragged themselves to the parapet to face the next attack.

It came with a desperate fury in a cloud of thundering hooves and blazing lead. It came in a storm of arrows and bullets, most of which did nothing but splinter the thick logs but some which found targets in living flesh. The sentry in the watch-tower screamed and toppled from his high platform. A man next to Mike grunted and fell, a feathered shaft in his neck. A third swore helplessly as a bullet smashed his right hand. Then the Indians were charging the walls and the air was heavy with the smoke and noise of battle.

Mike emptied his rifle at a succession

of painted faces, smashed down with the butt until the weapon was a broken ruin in his hands. A lithe warrior climbing the shoulders of his comrades, sprang over the parapet and sank his tomahawk into a soldier's skull. Another, screaming the war whoop of the Sioux, closed with a wounded man, struggled for a moment, then toppled from the firing platform, his teeth tearing at the white man's throat. In seconds, it seemed, one side of the fort was a screaming mass of shooting, killing Indians.

'We're beaten!' General Clarke, blood streaming from a long gash on his scalp, staggered back to the edge of the platform. Desperately he tore at his pistol as still more Indians climbed the stockade.

Mike dropped the ruined rifle, ran along the platform to a clear space then, turning, dropped his hands to the guns at his waist. The twin Colts cleared leather, his thumbs rolling back the hammers as he levelled the long barrels and, with grim efficiency, he began to shoot.

He adopted the gunfighters' stance, the pistols held at waist-height, his elbows bent, the heavy guns held before him. He fired with cold deliberation, knowing that accuracy was far more important than speed and, with every shot, a painted Indian screamed and died.

Ten times the Colts roared their flaming challenge and ten times a warrior of the Sioux toppled from the firing platform. Quickly the tall man reloaded, thrusting fresh cartridges into his guns and, as he did so, he became aware of the crack of rifles and the hum of bullets. He looked down and saw the general, together with the sergeant, sitting on top of one of the shacks, firing their rifles apparently directly at him.

But the bullets were aimed not to kill but to protect. The two rifles laid a curtain of death between him and the top of the parapet and three twitching

Indians showed that the protection had more than once saved his life.

Again the heavy Colts roared out their thunder, steadily, deliberately, bucking in the hands of a man who had learned the prime essential of any gunfighter. The stark necessity of knowing how to make the first shot, the important shot, hit its target. He wasted no shots, wasted no time, but each time he thumbed the hammers an Indian died.

For a moment the press of warriors hesitated, even the blood-crazed warriors hesitating about rushing to certain death. Then they rushed again, dropping over the stockade from a dozen points, yelling and screaming as they shot and stabbed at the dead and the wounded.

Mike, after one glance, jumped from the firing platform and raced across the compound. He saw the general and the sergeant shoot and club their way towards the office and, even as they reached it, the tall man dived towards the door.

'Guns! Quick!'

The sergeant thrust a pair of loaded Colts into his hands and again the staccato song of death echoed over the fort. Behind him both the general and the sergeant tore pistols from their racks, loaded them, set them to hand. Now was the time to conserve the last few bullets. Fire-power and fire-power alone could smash back the attack.

If it could be beaten back at all.

Smoke filled the compound, the smoke from the roaring guns and smoke from winking points of flame. The powder smoke rolled and billowed from the flaming muzzles of pistols fired, dropped, and then fired again as the general reloaded them. The winking points of flame began to spread, running along the dry, resin soaked timber.

And then, suddenly, the yelling mass of redskins headed back towards the stockade.

'They're on the retreat,' General

Clarke stared at the vanishing Indians. 'Why?'

'Don't waste time in talk.' Mike stepped from the shack, his guns heavy in his hands. He stared around the compound with red-rimmed eyes and then, as no Indians were to be seen, thrust the Colts into his holsters. 'Get those fires out.'

'Crazy!' The General snatched up a blanket and shook his head as he ran towards the fires. 'We were beaten, lost, and yet they ran away. I don't understand it.'

'Indians,' snapped Mike. 'They do some funny things. Let's get these fires out and then we'll take a look outside.'

Together they worked like madmen to beat out the flames. They smothered them with blankets, beat at them with tunics and harness, fought the flames as they had fought the Indians, with the grim resolve that they simply would not be beaten.

And because of that they won.

But the battle had cost them dear.

The compound was filled with dead, Indians and white men, tossed together in the final indignity of death. Of all the garrison only the sergeant, the general and Mike himself had survived. The buildings were burned and charred from the fires, the stockade splintered and the whole place stank of blood, gunsmoke and burning.

The Indians had won, and yet they had run off before making their victory complete.

The answer lay outside.

From the woods and over the plain men, dressed in the Union blue, galloped towards the fort. From them and from the fort itself the Indians rode away from the relief column at their heels. Red Arrow, cunning and wise in the ways of war, had yet made one great mistake. The relief column, spurred on by Sam and riding as few soldiers had ever ridden before, had arrived well before they had been expected.

Another hour and they would have arrived to see the fort a column of flame and smoke. An hour sooner and they would have caught the Indians between two fires. As it was they arrived just in time to save the three lone defenders and their coming reported by the Indian scouts, Red Arrow had withdrawn his warriors.

In that he was wise. The fort was tempting and he could have destroyed it, but forts could be rebuilt while Indian warriors were not expendable. So he had called off the attack and retreated.

'We've won!' The sergeant, almost hysterical with relief, laughed and waved towards the oncoming troops.

'We've won,' said the general. 'The fort is saved.'

'Yes,' said Mike. 'But if Sam had taken a little longer to carry the message, or if they had taken a little longer to arrive . . . ' He shrugged. It was just another incident in the way of life. The fort was saved, his life and those of the other two had been spared, but that was all. Others, many others, had died and for them the relief had arrived too late.

He leaned against the rough logs of the stockade and looked towards the advancing troops. This, he knew, was not the end. This was just the beginning, an isolated incident in the great Indian uprising which would rage throughout the middle west. The Sioux, now that the war-drums had echoed across the prairie, would make no easy peace. They would fight and kill and die to stop the railroad advancing into their land, to stop the buffalo hunters from robbing them of their food, the prospectors and traders from stealing their gold, their furs, and the dignity of their way of life with their rot-gut whiskey and double-dealing.

It was a war for survival and it would last until the final defeat of General Custer and the Little Big Horn.

But Mike did not know that. All he knew was that this was the beginning of the end. The beginning of total conquest for the white man and the end of Indian dominance.

For the Sioux, even while they fought, were heading towards extinction as a culture and a race. They would fight and they would lose their fight until, in the end, they would be herded like cattle on to a reservation.

There the remnants of the once-great Sioux would live — but the price of their survival would be utter and complete degradation.

And the sound of the war-drums over the prairie would be a thing heard only in the memories of old men.